I0671780

Grace and the Cowboy

by

Amity Grays

This is a work of fiction. Names, characters, places, and incidents are either the product of the author's imagination or are used fictitiously, and any resemblance to actual persons living or dead, business establishments, events, or locales, is entirely coincidental.

Grace and the Cowboy

COPYRIGHT © 2017 by Amity Grays

All rights reserved. No part of this book may be used or reproduced in any manner whatsoever without written permission of the author or The Wild Rose Press, Inc. except in the case of brief quotations embodied in critical articles or reviews.
Contact Information: info@thewildrosepress.com

Cover Art by *Kristian Norris*

The Wild Rose Press, Inc.
PO Box 708
Adams Basin, NY 14410-0708
Visit us at www.thewildrosepress.com

Publishing History
First Yellow Rose Edition, 2017
Print ISBN 978-1-5092-1523-2
Digital ISBN 978-1-5092-1524-9

Published in the United States of America

A plastic-covered blue book sat upon his dresser.

Now that was just sloppy, almost insulting, but...she'd take it.

Grace darted across the room. Grabbing the book, she slid it inside the robe's inner pocket. She felt like the Grinch, so very pleased and ever-so-slightly devious. Only she wasn't stealing from good little boys and girls. She was taking back stolen goods from a very naughty man. One who'd be returning very soon if the lack of running water was any indication.

Crap!

Her heart skipped a beat. She tensed, tilting her ear a little closer to the door. She didn't hear anyone coming, but that wouldn't be true for long.

She stormed out of his room just as the bathroom door opened and a towel-clad cowboy stepped out.

Grace froze, as did he. Their gazes met, her eyes widening with alarm as his narrowed with suspicion.

Fear shoved her pulse to racing even as her legs stood still. *Okay, this isn't going to end well.* Finally, impulse overrode terror, and she bolted for her room.

But Mac's arms folded around her long before she even made it halfway. Wet yet warm, solid yet soft, sexy yet...well, sexy stood alone—the man was hot, and by the look on his face, apparently steamed.

Faster than she could mark his intent, he had her spun around and headed right back into his room.

The door closed and a lock turned.

Dedication

To Mac.
This one's for you, babe.

Chapter One

Beneath a contemptuous snarl she couldn't have hidden to save her life, Grace Wade clenched her teeth together tighter than a pit bull's in the heat of battle. No way, absolutely *no way* would she spend the next several hours traveling anywhere with the unscrupulous heathen before her.

Turning her back to the smug look of amusement Mac Palmer wore so naturally across his face, she punched the last few numbers into her cell. All around her, inside the Dallas airport, people swarmed, some alone, many in groups. Several waited with loved ones who'd arrived to pick them up, their excited chatter buzzing in the air like a holiday celebration.

Nice for them.

What had she gotten? Lucifer himself, arriving in Wranglers, boots, and a monster-sized Texan ego. A quick glance back over her shoulder toward the luggage carousel assured her the rogue was still standing at least two full cowboy-strides away. Not far enough by her way of thinking, but at least he wasn't attempting to interfere.

She hated the fact she still found him attractive. Tall, tan, and as fit as a champion bull rider—her fantasies of finding him fat, dumpy, and haggard by the harsh Texas elements were now officially blown beyond any kind of use.

Honestly, could time afford her no mercy?

It had been four years. The scoundrel hadn't even had the decency to let his hair start thinning. Oh no, Mac still toted the same full and alluring head of loose, sand-colored curls he always had. The kind a girl couldn't help but want to run through her fingers.

"Stupid genetics," she mumbled before looking away. That was one strike against biology if ever there was one. By her way of thinking, a snake should look like a snake no matter what his DNA.

The annoying sound of another unanswered ring played in her ear. There was a chance her grandfather was out with his men, but she doubted it. His years of early rising had ended several years back. The old codger was probably avoiding her.

Yeah, that she could believe.

"Hello."

Hallelujah!

"Grandpa? Grandpa, it's Grace. Look, I'm not riding back with—"

"You've reached the Wade residence. No one is available to take your call at this time. Please hang up and try your call again later."

"You've got to be kidding me. Grandpa, I know it's you. Do not hang up the—"

The line went dead.

The cantankerous old goat actually hung up on her.

Grace held out the cell in strangulation style, shaking the gadget threateningly as she searched for a place to throw it. Her gaze landed on the perfect target, but her nerve was hampered by the knowledge Mac would likely catch the flying device and take the pleasure of smashing it himself. His luck, as well as his audacity, had been serving as a reliable thorn in her side for years.

As though reading her mind, the cowboy pushed back his Stetson and smiled.

Attraction and fury danced a duel down her spine. She'd forgotten the potency of that smoldering hot grin.

Could the man be any more annoying?

Grace stared back at the cell. Yes, yes he could. He had, after all, been taking lessons from the best—her grandfather. Dear old Grandpa had perfected the art of annoyance years ago.

Luckily, she'd learned a thing or two from him herself.

With fierce determination, she punched back in the numbers. A deep chuckle sounded from behind. Mac knew her grandfather well and knew exactly what she was up against—a fact which cranked the cords of her tightly wired nerves near to springing.

Hoping a look could indeed kill, she swung back around and cast the cowboy the best six-foot-under glare she could possibly muster. By all appearances unaffected, Mac drew a weary breath as he took off his Stetson and raked his hands through those scrumptious curls.

Sexy.

Stupid, unfair, deceptive genetics.

Walking away from him and the luggage carousel, Grace crossed the terminal to the Rent-A-Ride kiosk. The last thing she needed was another reminder of how potent the man could be. She got it. She'd always gotten it. But she also understood that behind the handsome exterior beat the heart of a rat.

The best way—no, the *only* way—to handle Mac

Palmer was to stay away, a plan she'd put in place four years back and had no intention of veering from now.

That was, if she could set her grandfather straight.

The phone rang and rang, finally forcing her to hang up. Not at all deterred, she dialed again. "Stubborn, pig-headed, old man," she declared just as her grandfather picked up.

"The apple doesn't fall far from the tree, little lady. Now, quit whining about your druthers, and get your hiney out here."

"Don't hang up!" she said in a rush, turning around to make sure Mac hadn't followed. He hadn't, but wanting to make sure he deciphered not a word, she covered her lips and the mouthpiece before letting loose her frustrations. "What were you thinking, Grandpa? I asked you to get rid of the man, and instead, you send him to fetch me. Is that any way to treat your only grandchild? I mean…really, did you give it *any* thought?"

"I'm not going to fire Mac. He's the best hand I've ever had, not to mention this is his home. One of these days the ranch will be his. I can hardly give him the axe."

The loud hum of the terminal forced her to raise her voice, but she kept her back averted, covering her intentions the best she could. "I never said to fire him. I said get rid of him. You can do it any way you see fit— a vacation, a task, a long trip off the short end of a dock. I don't care how you do it. I just want him gone."

"He stays. Get over it. The man's the real deal— honorable, hardworking, trustworthy. Never knew a man who could muster cattle like him. The men respect him. I respect him. I have no idea what it is you have against him, other than the fact he's Garrett's brother—a fact, by the way, not a sin. Now, get yourself out here and quit wasting mine and Mac's time."

"But I—"

The buzz of an ended conversation played through the line. She stared at the cell. All her friends had sweet, loving grandfathers who adored them. What happened to hers?

Mac Palmer—she had plenty against the man. He had single-handedly ruined her life. And from what she could tell, he'd taken a great deal of pleasure in doing it.

Slowly dropping the phone to her side, she turned back around to face him. Still standing where he'd been the entire time, looking a little peeved, but otherwise undaunted, Mac placed his hat back on his head and nodded toward the carousel that was now turning.

Really? He intended to rush her?

She marched back across the terminal—head held high, shoulders back, focus set, and stride determined. Yeah, she was ready all right—ready to call foul and catch the next bird out. She had only one destination in mind: home—Vancouver, British Columbia, where her grandmother would be waiting with open arms. Mac could stand there and watch or he could leave. Either way, the end result would be the same. She would not tolerate any further manipulation in her life, not by him, not by her grandfather.

"Ready?" he asked as she approached.

Storming past him, her slightly elevated pumps tap, tap, tapping her resolve, she met her somewhat peculiar assortment of luggage as it dropped from the shoot. First her grandmother's large, aged, burlap and leather case, which at one time, years ago, would have been labeled extravagant. Today, it could best be defined as cumbersome. Next to drop was the smaller, white-and-pink, umbrella-holding-flamingo-printed suitcase borrowed from her grandmother's rather flamboyant neighbor, Myrtle Poundstone. Both were a necessity, as she'd discovered the morning of her departure that her own rather expensive set of luggage, which she'd lent to a friend a month prior, was taking a cruise of the Caribbean.

Trying her best to pull off dignity while toting the ridiculous entourage, she marched right back past Mac toward the ticket counter on the opposite side of the airport. Her stay in the States was officially over.

His steady strides were captured and reported in the even clicks of his boots against the tiled floor.

Fine, let him follow. Let him try and stop me. Let him—

The handles she held slipped from her fingers as the suitcases were tugged back the opposite direction.

What?

Mouth gaping, she maneuvered a quick U-turn. Mac had hold of her luggage and was headed toward the exit.

"Hey," she shouted. The fast and determined clicks of his boots were soon echoed by the frantic taps of her shoes. "Wait! Stop. Hold on just a minute."

He disappeared into the sky bridge linking the terminal with the parking garage, widening the distance between them with his long and unmerciful strides.

She hurried behind him, dodging those arriving while doing her best to keep her gaze on the madman stealing her bags.

At the end of the bridge, he took another right and made his way across a packed lot. Already huffing and puffing, Grace quickened her steps into a run, finally catching up with him as he ascended a ramp toward the next level.

"Give me back my bags. You're such an—" Her ankle twisted somewhat. She stumbled but managed to right herself.

The oaf didn't even pretend to slow down.

A group of teenage boys headed their way. "Stop him," she screamed, pointing to the long-legged cowboy. "He's stolen my bags."

The teens eyed him warily.

"Temper tantrum," Mac explained with a nod over his shoulder.

The deep Texas drawl she'd once found so alluring hit her nerves like an electrical rod.

The group simply shook their heads, grunting their understanding.

"Nice luggage," one of the young men chimed in before smirking her way as he and his gangly posse moved past her.

"Really?" She vented her indignation. "That's the extent of your chivalry? I'm sure your parents would be *sooooo* proud."

The boys merely laughed, the mouthy one throwing a "Good luck, buddy" in Mac's direction.

Left with no choice but to follow the thief as he moved from the ramp and across the lot, Grace soon found herself heading toward a white, four-door sedan.

She halted dead in her tracks. "I am not getting in that car."

Mac stopped beside the sedan, opened the back

door, and tossed in her luggage.

"What's wrong with you?" she demanded. "Do you have some kind of caveman complex, or are you simply trying to make me miserable? Keep my luggage for all I care. It's not like there's anything there I can't replace."

After closing the door, he turned and headed back her way.

"Why do you have to be such a jerk? I'm not…" She paused and swallowed. He came across as slightly intimidating with his long, purposeful strides and no-nonsense demeanor closing in on her. "I'm not going with you." Her words ran fast, and her pitch rang a bit too high as she took a couple steps back.

Mac stopped directly in front of her. Eyes she knew to be a steely-blue were shadowed by the bridge of his hat, hiding from her his intent. The next thing she knew, he'd snatched her purse—which held her funds as well as her passport—from her shoulder and tucked it under his arm.

Stunned stupid, she could do nothing but watch as he turned back around and headed for the car. The man *was* a beast—far worse than she remembered.

As the shock faded, determination set in. Grace charged after him, not making it to his side until he had the passenger door open. She ignored the invitation and grabbed for her purse.

He simply held it out of her reach. "Let me tell you how this is going to work," he said, his voice low but thick with held temper. "You're going to start behaving and get inside the car, dignity intact, or I'm going to throw you in kicking and screaming."

She gasped.

"I'm not much for game playing, Grace. I suggest

you crawl in."

Her body shook with rage. She could practically feel her nerve endings coiling. Only once before in her life had she been so angry she could cry, and just like now, it had been this man's smug face which kept her from it.

Though she longed, with every ounce of her being, to slap the arrogant expression right off his face, she instead held her fury in check and moved, albeit, rather rigidly, into the car.

"Buckle up," he instructed.

Crossing her arms over her chest, she fought the impulse to attack.

"Either you do it, or I will."

His combative words, delivered with his deep tone and don't-tempt-me Texas twang, nearly sent her lunging for his throat. Unable to completely check the urge, she opted to let words deliver the actual strike. "Just so we're perfectly clear. I'd rather ride beside a nasty rattler than the likes of *you*."

"Is that so?" He reached across her lap to pull forward her belt. "Lucky for you, I'm a little shy on the critters. Because, believe me, at the moment, I'd happily oblige you your preference."

Once again, the rim of his cowboy hat hid his face and thankfully her reaction. Shock purged any would-have-been retort right from her lips. But it wasn't the shock of his words. Those hadn't surprised her in the slightest. He'd always been a disagreeable man. No, it was her reaction to his physical presence that jolted her speechless.

How could his scent strike such a strong chord? Masculine—she wasn't entirely sure how she'd define it past that point. It seemed completely mutinous that her senses could betray her in such a way, embracing his scent as though he were actually safe to breathe.

A click signaled the belt secure. The hat tilted up, and his mesmerizing eyes stared into hers. "You'll want to leave that in place." His left hand slid around the buckle, brushing against her middle as he pulled the belt tight with his right.

Dozens of sensations she refused to analyze suddenly stirred throughout her body.

His eyes sparked with mischief as he checked the belt's hold. "I have a feeling it's going to be a bumpy ride."

Heaven help him, the woman hadn't changed, still as head-strong and unreasonable as ever. If Mac would've had any kind of wits about him, he'd have refused Eldon's request and let the old man pick up his own bound-to-be-a-problem employee.

As the sedan sped down the road toward the smaller airstrip just outside of Dallas, he snuck a peek in Grace's direction. Blonde highlights ran thick through long, light-brown hair, making it hard to decide which category to place her. Thick lashes, which had, to his memory, never seen a lick of mascara, framed eyes now closed—eyes still strikingly blue.

Instinctively, his gaze moved lower. The body he remembered as flawless had somehow managed to blossom into an even more alluring form. Unforgettable curves had developed into a masterpiece of feminine perfection, distracting enough to pull even the most diligent of cowboys off the beaten trail, even those who knew the temptress came loaded with enough attitude to send them over a ledge.

Curse my luck. If possible, she'd only grown more beautiful over the last four years. Between her try-and-take-your-eyes-off-this swing and determined insolence, Grace Wade was going to be a hard one to ignore, and that was the only plan he'd managed to configure since realizing he was still a bee in her bonnet.

Ignoring her was a talent he'd unfortunately lost shortly out of his teens, right around the time she'd decided he wasn't worth her efforts. Served him right of course; he'd been less than careful with her young, infatuated heart.

He'd been bitter back then. Distraught over the loss of his father, he hadn't cared much about her feelings, too young to understand what an effect his behavior would have, and too numb himself to care how badly he would one day regret it.

Leaning her head back against the seat's rest, she appeared momentarily at peace. With her many guards down, she looked a bit like an angel—a side of Grace he hadn't seen for years. Typically, she entered his presence guard up, fists raised.

Why had he ever imagined, even for a moment, he should break the news to her, let her know the man she loved had left her for another? He should've made Garrett stand up and be the man Mac always knew he could be.

He should have, but he hadn't.

Swallowing, he returned his attention to the path before him, cursing the memories that still clung as though fresh in the back of his mind. He'd do anything to take it back, to allow time to do her mending instead of trying to bandage her himself. The last thing he'd wanted to do was hurt her further. He'd gone to the hotel that night to let her down easy, to help her see Garrett's decision had actually been for the best.

Fool.

He'd been a fool then, and he was still a fool today.

Who was he trying to kid? Eldon hadn't forced him into anything. He'd wanted to pick Grace up, wanted to see her. Spend the few hours alone with her. He'd hoped things had changed, that she'd realized marrying Garrett would have been a mistake, and in doing so, forgiven him.

A fool's dream.

She'd never forgive him, not for any of it. Her resentment went much deeper than time alone could heal.

He wondered why she'd even bothered to come. She obviously was more than willing to turn tail and go home, so her agreement with her grandfather couldn't be that mentally binding. Perhaps her grandmother, Patsy, had forced her hand.

Mac smiled. Yeah, he'd bet a pretty penny that was exactly what happened.

Grace opened her eyes and shifted in her seat, pulling lower the skirt which had climbed to show off a good three inches of her unforgettable thighs. "What are you so happy about?" she asked, her tone reflecting her disfavor.

Yep, the shrew has awakened.

"Actually, I was thinking about Patsy. How is she?" It wasn't just a way to break the silence. He was genuinely fond of Eldon's estranged wife. She'd been an important part of his life for years, always making sure he and Garrett were well cared for when their mother's early bouts of despair left her nearly unable to cope.

Grace shifted again, scooting herself as far away from him as possible. He could feel her heated glare; he saw no reason to turn and acknowledge it.

"Look," he said, giving his best shot at the so-called higher ground, "we don't have to be friends. But it's a long trip between here and Buster's Prairie. We may as well be civil."

"Hah!" she blurted before turning to look out her side window.

Her lips were held tight, but he could almost hear the numerous insults held behind their guard.

Grunting, he took a firm grip on the wheel. "I see nothing's changed."

"That's right," she said with true derision. "You're still the ass you've always been."

Her plenty-pleased expression, reflected in the glass, worked well as a punch to his patience. "Oh no, sweetheart, you don't get to do that."

The image of a questioning brow bounced back his direction from the window. "I have no idea what you're talking about, but it really doesn't matter as I'm not talking to you anyway." Shaking her head in a gesture similar to shaking off an unpleasant thought, she added, "And don't call me sweetheart."

"You don't get to break your silence only to throw nasty remarks, which by the way, still equates to talking."

Sighing, she leaned back in her seat and closed her eyes, by all appearances, checking out. But she surprised him with, "Grandmother's fine. She said to tell you hello and…" Her top lip twitched.

"And?"

She sat silent a moment. "She sends her love."

He almost smiled at the way her lips snarled around the word as though she'd tasted something bitter. "I've missed Patsy," he confessed. "I half-expected to find her at the airport with you."

"I'm twenty-five years old. Quite capable of flying the big blue skies on my own. Why would my grandmother come along? This is my debt, not hers."

"This is her home. With you no longer in Vancouver, I thought maybe she'd finally return."

She remained quiet for some time. It dawned on him how carefully she was selecting her words. A stark difference from the woman he had known. Words were one thing Grace Wade had never guarded.

Releasing a heavy breath, she looked down to her joined hands. "Vancouver is her home, born and raised. Texas is my grandfather's home."

"She's Eldon's wife. That makes it her home as well."

Her perfectly arched brows bumped into a scowl. "They haven't seen each other in four years. I believe it's all right to acknowledge they're over."

Turning back to the path ahead, he looked somewhere past the green pastures and grazing cattle that lined both sides of the freeway and nodded. She was right, though it was a truth he seldom visited. Maybe because Eldon still spoke of Patsy as though she were his. In fact, Mac would bet his last dollar the old man was still waiting for her, probably never actually assuming she'd continue to stay away.

A quick glance across his shoulder to Grace showed her feelings weren't as dry to the matter as her words had indicated.

"I imagine you're right," he acknowledged. "Though, I've never understood why she and Eldon couldn't simply work things out. They obviously still love each other."

Her arresting blue eyes widened with surprise. "Why would you think that? They couldn't be in the same room together for more than twenty minutes without bickering."

He shrugged his shoulders. It seemed obvious to him. "If they didn't still love each other, one of them would have filed for divorce, don't you think?"

"Divorce is no different than marriage." The same heavy scowl reappeared between her brows. "It's just a stupid piece of paper."

This took him aback. She sounded so serious. Nothing like the girl who'd dreamt of getting married from the young age of eight. Nor the woman who'd meticulously planned and then re-planned her wedding every time his brother moved back the date.

Somewhere along the line, the hopeless romantic had died. It saddened him more than a little knowing he'd most likely contributed to her death.

"I know marriage still means something to Eldon." He kept his gaze on the long road ahead as his thoughts wandered back to his friend and the one truth time had not changed. "I know he still loves her. He talks about her all the time, misses her horribly. I've heard him on the phone to you. Haven't you ever noticed how he always turns the conversation around to your grandmother? How he always has a reason he must talk to her when you call? Lame reasons, I might add."

Her silence sparked his curiosity. He shot a quick

glance her way, catching her pursing her lips while apparently giving his words some thought.

A quick bite into her lower lip and she looked back his way. "I have noticed."

Mac smiled. "He wants to hear her voice. He needs to know she's all right. He's hoping to capture some hope. In fact…" He hesitated, not certain how she'd feel about the theory.

"In fact, what?"

"I'm guessing by forcing you to live up to your obligation, Eldon is hoping it will bring her back."

"Maybe." She turned a bit too late to hide the sadness in her eyes. "Still, I think when there's nothing to salvage it's best for everyone to move on. Otherwise, you're merely replaying the same mistakes, producing the same outcome, hurting way too many people along the way."

She wasn't speaking of Eldon and Patsy.

"Grace, tell me you haven't been counseling Patsy."

"I'm not going to lie to my grandmother."

"It's not Patsy you're lying to, but that doesn't mean it's not hurting her."

"Don't," she said, the sorrow in her voice nearly tearing him in two. "*You* don't get to lecture me on hurting others."

A heavy weight fell upon his heart. He spared her a quick glance. "I never wanted to hurt you. That was never what it was about."

"Seriously? You never thought it would hurt me? He was my fiancé. I thought we were going to be married. I'd planned my entire life around him. I loved Garrett."

"Maybe you did, but that doesn't—"

"No." She raised her hands. "Anything we had to say to each other, we said four years ago."

"Grace, I—"

"Not another word." Her fiery glare met his gaze in the window's reflection.

What could he do? He looked back to the road. "Fine, if that's the way you want it."

"It is."

Silence punctuated the agreement clear to the airstrip.

Chapter Two

Opening the glass door a tad wider, Grace leaned in to absorb the refreshing feel of cool.

Ah...

Closing her eyes, she happily embraced the comfort. The grind of a motor working hard droned above her head as the cool air swarmed around her. The quick jaunt to the Arctic was a welcomed relief from the blistering Texas heat. And though she would have dearly loved to stay longer, she knew the cost of the trip was being born by another.

Opening her eyes, she scanned the refrigerator's parameter and caught sight of a familiar red can. She grabbed the soda then closed the door and took a look around. Sitting at the edge of the airstrip about forty-five minutes outside of Dallas, the conveniently placed mini-mart would be her last chance for a meal before boarding the four-passenger Cessna which would take them to the ranch.

She could hear Mac talking with the cashier at the front of the store as she searched the aisles for something to eat. Since her captor had confiscated her purse, he would be buying, which, by her way of thinking, meant the sky was the limit.

She smiled.

Crackers, chips, candy bars—she was starved, so they all looked good but hardly made a meal.

"Grace, over here," Mac hollered, spotting her near the end of the aisle and waving her over to the checkout. He pointed to the rotary warmers lining the counter opposite the register. "It's four hours to home. You'll want to fill up."

Thanking him with a mock salute, she moved around the counter and began perusing her options—corn dogs, hot dogs, chili dogs, sausage. None sounded too good a plan if the next stop lay four hours away. She opted for a corndog, or "Pluto Pup" as the sign read, and chips with melted cheese.

"The dinner of champs," she said, placing her selections down beside his on the counter.

Eying their fair, he grimaced. "Not a lot of choices this route, I'm afraid." Opening his wallet, he dropped payment on the counter. After thanking the merchant, he nodded toward the two booths sitting empty near the back of the store. "After you, sweetheart."

She sauntered out in front of him, tossing a glance over her shoulder as she moved. "Don't call me sweetheart."

The endearment, uttered with that sexy, Texas drawl, was nothing but infuriating for its appeal. Every time she heard it, she wondered just how many "sweethearts" the man had.

Mac had always been quite the looker. Blessed with features falling easily into the category of ruggedly handsome, he never failed to turn heads. If his adorable curls didn't wrap themselves around a woman's interest, then those breathtaking eyes always did the trick. Topped by dark, masculine brows that contrasted, yet complemented well, the dark blond of his hair, they were nothing short of arresting. Usually a steely-blue, his eyes could turn as dark as the night, changing drastically at times to follow his moods—bright when humored, smoky when distracted, piercing when angry, and dark when aroused. She'd seen them all, but it was visions of the latter that had visited her often over the last four years.

Their last meeting had been fierce, filled with raw emotions laid bare by careless words. But there had been something else brewing in the fire that raged between them, something primal and new. Its truth had flashed in his eyes, quieted her tongue, and danced for a charged moment inside a space that had, until then, only seen battle. They'd both startled and stepped apart, the war over with no victor declared.

That had been the last time she'd seen him, but she'd never forgotten those eyes.

What rotten luck that memory could carry so well across the miles.

Grace stopped directly in front of the first booth and eyed the crumb-covered table with skepticism. She'd have moved on, but the next table down didn't look any better.

"Like I said, not a lot of choices this route," Mac reminded, stepping around her and brushing the crumbs to the side. He then waited for her to slide into the first seat before taking the one directly across from her.

That about summed up their relationship, as pathetic as it was. They were always sitting on opposite sides. She smiled, though not certain she should feel so amused.

"Want to share the joke?" he asked, helping himself to one of her cheese-covered chips.

"Why did the cowboy cross the road?"

Mac watched her silently a moment as though leery of walking into a trap. Taking off his hat, he placed it down on the seat beside him. "All right, why?"

"To sit on the opposite side." Laughing, she grabbed her corndog and loaded it with mustard. "I crack myself up."

Those blue eyes turned dark as they narrowed with suspicion. Another look she knew well. Suspicion, annoyance, disdain—he'd worn the expression often around her, and from a very young age. She'd simply rubbed the boy he had been the wrong way, a truth which carried forward to the man.

Despite endless attempts to win him over, she never was able to change his opinion to her favor. Looking back, she felt a complete fool for having tried so ridiculously hard for so ridiculously long. It was those stupid genetics again, making him hard to resist and making her unreasonably bound and determined.

She'd been absolutely heart-over-common-sense in love with the thirteen-year-old boy who rode horses like none she had ever seen. She'd often heard it said he was born for the saddle, and that wasn't so hard to believe. Mac Palmer was an absolutely breathtaking sight upon a horse and always had been.

But that wasn't what won her young heart. He'd won that even before their first hello. Shockingly handsome, even back then, she was instantly attracted. But it wasn't his looks that so completely drew her in. It was his stance, his somewhat reserved demeanor that truly intrigued her. For whatever the reason, she'd felt them kindred spirits.

Yeah, right.

His reaction to her had been slightly less

favorable—snide, short, at times simply rude. His complete disinterest and later disdain had set in her a determination she never overcame. Luckily, the determination changed forms through the years as her attraction for him turned to anger and resentment. She figured if she was bound to annoy him, she may as well put some effort into it. Spiteful retorts, blatant defiance—attempts, in general, to make his life miserable. Insolence became such an instinctual way of responding, it lingered well past the time the defense was actually needed.

Grabbing another richly endowed chip, Mac continued to stare her way. "You've changed," he said before shoving the entire chip into his mouth.

"For the better or for the worse?" she asked, wishing instantly she could take it back. She didn't care about his opinion, not at all. Grabbing a chip herself, she nibbled on it slowly, waiting more anxiously than a person of indifference should.

"Too early to tell." He leaned back farther in the booth, studying her boldly.

Most likely, he was picking her apart, counting her numerous flaws, forming conclusions unflattering at best. Feeling no need to await his verdict, she looked away to load once more her feast on a stick.

"So, Grace, that's an interesting set of luggage you're toting."

Though she was thankful for the change in topic, she still eyed him warily. "Your point being?"

"Come on, there has to be a story."

"There is."

He grinned. "All right, I'll admit I'm curious, but I'm not going to beg."

Of course he wouldn't. Mac Palmer never begged for anything. He never had to.

"My luggage is currently traveling the world with my friend's mother."

He tilted his genetically over-blessed head. "And what—you got the pink flamingos in some kind of trade? Dang, Grace, remind me to keep you out of any bartering."

Letting out a heavy sigh, she mimicked his posture and leaned back against her seat. "The burlap case belongs to my grandmother. The flamingos belong to our neighbor, Myrtle Poundstone. She's into the creatures. In fact, she has their replicated forms, dressed in various fashions, strategically placed throughout her yard."

Mac cringed.

Grace laughed. "It gets better. Guess what she surprised Grandma with last spring?"

"Oh, no."

"Oh, yes. I think it literally pains her, but our very own plaid-clad flamingo sits a little less than proudly out near our garbage cans."

Mac laughed as he nodded. "Also strategically placed?"

"I'm certain she's hoping the garbage men mistake it for trash one day. But so far, no such luck."

His blue eyes shined bright with humor. "Patsy always was too kind for her own good."

"Yes, she has a big heart."

The silence that followed was oddly peaceful. With smiles sitting comfortably on both their faces, they could have easily been mistaken for old friends. And they might have been, had things been different, had she not fallen for him so hard, had he responded more kindly.

Slightly taken aback by the truth of it, Grace swallowed and looked away.

Mac reached for another chip. "So, why'd you lend out your luggage when you knew you were going to need it?"

She looked back, noting that behind his narrowed lids, his eyes now looked a bit haunted. Had he felt it, too? Realized, like her, how different things could have been?

Probably not. He most likely never thought that much about her.

"Actually, I loaned them to my friend Sarah about a month back. Then, due to our schedules never quite meshing, I never got the pieces back. Her mother asked her a week ago if she could borrow her luggage. Sarah said yes, thinking she meant only her two small bags. She never thought twice about it until she went to bring me my suitcases and found they were gone."

"And you didn't have time to go shopping?"

"I barely had time to borrow replacements. My plane was leaving that afternoon."

He took a long breath, his gaze never leaving hers. "You're here for two years, Grace. You waited to pack until the last minute?"

"I was busy."

She had procrastinated, dragged her feet, hoping fate would step in and relinquish her from a responsibility her conscience would not. It wasn't that she didn't want to see her grandfather or love the ranch. She did.

It was the humiliation she wanted to avoid—the

thousand plus "this was your life" memories depicting her as the desperate maiden. She'd worked very hard over the last few years to forget what a fool she'd been and gain back a protective layer of self-respect. The station held a thirteen-year-collection of Grace Wade's most embarrassing moments and dismal failings. She feared what small layer of self-respect she'd built would crumble when faced with the truth of her past.

Pathetic. She could think of no other word for it.

After years of being brushed off by the love of her pre-teen life, she had, at the age of fourteen, finally surrendered and moved on. But she hadn't moved far. Only a few years later, it was Garrett, Mac's younger brother, who next won her heart.

As handsome as his older brother, but far more gentle a soul, Garrett's reaction to her had been entirely different. He'd adored her, followed her everywhere, and promised her forever.

Of course, no one could be held to a promise they made when they were so young.

Somewhere along that path to forever, she'd felt him drift away. Whether it was due to a change in him, a change in her, or the constant reiteration of his brother's many doubts, she still didn't know for sure. It had happened slowly; so slowly, it was now hard to look back and know exactly when it had begun. And back then, she hadn't wanted to see it. She'd lived a long time in denial, terrified of letting go. Garrett Palmer had become more to her than someone to love. He'd become her rock, her future, the security she so craved. She'd been certain her world would shatter without him.

Sneaking a peek across the table to Mac, she tried

to remember if Garrett's eyes were so captivating. It seemed odd she couldn't remember.

Mac finished his sausage then helped himself to another chip. "How are your folks?"

"Good. They're thinking of retiring and starting a nursery."

"No kidding?" He paused with the chip just outside his lips. "I never thought I'd see that day."

She shrugged her shoulders. "And you haven't yet. I personally will have to see it to believe it. They've always had these wild ideas of settling down, but then another unimaginable find is made and off they go with their team of eager past-collectors. I doubt that will change."

"They certainly love what they do." He glanced away slightly and nodded. "It really is pretty interesting," he added before looking back. "It wouldn't be for me, but I remember always being fascinated by their stories."

"They have some pretty good ones." She scowled as he grabbed for yet another chip. "Are you done eating my meal, or are you going to buy me another tray?" Grabbing one for herself, she shoved the whole thing into her mouth.

The handsome rogue merely grinned. "If you'd like."

Realizing the entire loaded chip had probably been a bad idea, she tried to appear something less than an idiot as she worked the uncomfortable size around in her mouth, chewing and swallowing in smaller, workable bites. She cleared her throat with a swig of soda. "How'd you feel about your mom marrying Doc Hamby?"

"Jason's a good guy." He shrugged his shoulders. "Mom seems happy."

"Yeah, she does, but that's not what I asked."

Mac's head tilted slightly as his hand moved behind it to rub against his neck. "You've stayed in contact with my mother?"

It sounded a bit accusatory.

"We exchange cards, add brief notes. Is that a problem?"

His brows lifted. "No." He shook his head, and the sun's rays lit the turns of his ever-so-sexy curls. "I'm merely surprised she never mentioned it."

"Why, because all things must go through the lord of the clan, Mac Palmer?"

His brow pulled into a scowl. "I simply would've thought she'd say something. And to answer your question, I'm very happy for my mother. She's been through a lot. She deserves to find happiness."

"That's very gracious of you—giving your blessing and all. I hear it's not an easy thing to come by."

"Grace—"

She'd delivered her punch. It was now time to tiptoe out of the ring. "Did they get married in Hawaii?"

His scrutinizing gaze suggested he recognized her strategy. "They got married at the ranch. She didn't tell you?"

"Nope. Just got a picture with a note saying Dr. and Mrs. Jason Hamby. They were standing in front of a group of palm trees with leis around their necks."

"They were married at the ranch then left a week later to Hawaii for their honeymoon." Mac sighed and shook his head. "I'm surprised Eldon didn't mention

27

it."

"He doesn't talk about the ranch or its happenings. He's usually too busy making digs at my grandmother in hopes I'll relay them."

"And do you?"

"Of course not. I simply say he sends his love."

Mac chuckled, the same deep, sexy chuckle she remembered from years past. "That would piss off the old gator," he noted, seeming genuinely amused.

"The old gator wouldn't know what was good for him if it arrived with bells and whistles."

"No, I don't imagine he would." Lifting his napkin, Mac wiped his lips. "I still have to square up the bill for the fuel. You can either join me or"—he nodded down to the remaining chips—"you can finish those and then meet me outside."

She leaned back against her seat. "Really, I have your permission? Wow. That means so much to me."

"I may change my mind if you keep insisting on being a smart aleck." Steel-blue eyes flashed with challenge and maybe a touch of playfulness.

Excitement sparked from somewhere deep within the regions of her self-imposed no-go zone. "Go," she said abruptly, batting her hand away toward the distance, shooing him as though he were a pesky fly. It was nothing short of scary how easily he could light her fire.

She'd really hoped that particular ignition switch had corroded over and died.

He grabbed his still uneaten hotdog and another chip as he scooted out of the booth. "Thanks, sweetheart," he drawled with a teasing grin.

Grace took a deep breath and gnawed on her

bottom lip as she watched him walk away. Ignoring Mac was proving more difficult than she'd expected. Turning in the booth toward the window, she grabbed another chip and continued to watch him as he walked across the asphalt to the large metal hangar, downing the rest of his meal as though he hadn't a care in the world.

He'd always had that smooth, I've-got-it-handled stride. Like everything else about the man, it was hard not to admire. She just didn't get it. How could a man who'd purposefully done nothing but bring her misery draw her like he did?

And he did. She couldn't deny it.

Even while she was with Garrett there had been that disturbing sense of awareness. She'd always known when he'd walked into a room, always known when he was watching her.

Maybe it was merely the tension built through years of heated emotions. They'd clashed and clashed regularly. She'd called it dislike, but in truth, mere disfavor rarely drew such strong responses. More than likely, it was the same unwanted nuisance that had plagued her as a young girl—a basic, body-over-mind attraction. One she could fight but never really beat.

It explained that night in Amarillo when their vicious fight had raged into an entirely unexpected spark…a startling, intense, mutually ignited spark.

Luckily, he'd taught her well through the years that attraction meant nothing.

So he was hot. So he'd found her desirable in that one bizarre, emotionally charged moment. Neither meant a thing. She'd simply been lost and distraught and not anywhere near herself, and he'd…well, Mac had been his typical, arrogant male self. Mix it all together and poof! Like the perfect measurements of vinegar and baking soda, there was bound to be a spark.

That didn't mean they belonged together.

And *they* most certainly didn't.

Mac was her enemy, tested and proven. Case in point—he'd spent months talking her fiancé out of marrying her. He'd been there at the hotel that night for one reason and one reason only—to let her know he had won. His brother didn't love her. He'd found another and moved on.

And so did she after that—moved on. On and away. Away from the awkwardness that was bound to arise between her and Mac. Away from the pitying looks her broken engagement would bring. Away from a ranch full of memories, hopes, and dreams shattered. But most of all, away from the foolish young woman she'd been, a woman she never again wanted to be.

No longer hungry, Grace scooted from the booth, grabbing the box of cheese-covered chips as she moved then tossing them in the garbage on her way out the door.

****

"Doing okay?" Mac hollered over the roar of the engine. For the most part, it had been an easy flight, but a couple strong gusts had just given them a jolt.

"I'm all right," Grace yelled back. "It's actually rather nice up here, even if a little loud."

"A little," he shouted back, and they both smiled.

The last few miles to Buster's Prairie were without a doubt the most enjoyable. Below them, long stretches of dry river beds tumbled into grass-covered flatlands broken midway through by an active stream fed from distant hills. The land was the richest in the area, perfect for cultivation and unmatched for grazing. Mac considered himself the luckiest man alive to be heir to such a land.

Thank God for his mother's determination and Eldon's willingness to go along.

It had been part of the agreement, written into the sale of Buster's Prairie. Upon sale, Mac and Garrett were to be given first rights of purchase. Thankfully, his mother had invested their inheritance well; though most credit, in truth, belonged to Eldon and Patsy's guidance.

"Are we close to the falls?" Grace asked, staring out the plane's side window, enjoying the view.

"They're just ahead." And a little to the east, but she wouldn't have to know. If a pass by the cliffs would make her happy, he'd gladly make the detour.

The small plane took another jolt, but her gaze never shifted from the scene below. "I'd forgotten how beautiful it could be," she shouted. "The hills, the plains…even the isolation has a certain kind of appeal." She let out a sad kind of laugh before shaking her head. "But I never forgot the falls. I'd try to describe them to those back home, but it was hard to capture its beauty with mere words. I'll have to take pictures this time." Looking his way, she asked, "Do you still ride out there often?"

"Not so much these days. With Garrett gone, the ranch keeps me pretty busy. I'll take rides with Eldon now and again, but he's limited in what he can do."

"Limited?"

"Age is catching up with him. In his mind, he's still young, but his body no longer tolerates long bouts on horseback, and especially not on bikes."

She remained silent a long moment, leaving the loud hum of the engine to take center stage.

He shot a quick glance her way. "Something wrong?"

She swallowed and met his gaze. "It's just…he still sounds so resilient. I never picture him growing old."

Mac looked back out toward the now approaching hills. "He's still stubborn and determined. He knows what's happening, but he refuses to acknowledge it. So he pushes himself…more than he should. Look over there." He pointed to a couple horses making their way to the stream. He took the plane lower to get a better view.

Grace scooted closer to the window. "Are they ours?"

"Nope."

"Are they wild?"

"I don't believe there are any wild horses left in Texas. None I've heard about anyway. They've either gotten away from their owners or they've been let loose."

"Let loose?"

"It seems to be happening more and more these days. People can't afford to feed their horses, so they drop them out on an open or private range believing they'll somehow take care of themselves. Sometimes the horses get lucky. Sometimes they don't. These seem to be in pretty good shape, too good of shape, actually. They've probably just gotten loose."

"Have you ever had them show up here before?"

"Only one other time about a year ago. There were three of them."

"What happened to those?"

"They'd been neglected, so we notified the Bureau of Land Management. They never did find their owners. We ended up adopting one of them, and the bureau sold the other two online to someone in Nevada."

He marked the general location then pulled the plane back high into the blue and continued on toward the falls.

Grace shifted in her seat to look his way. "They're such beautiful animals. I can't believe anyone would just let them go."

"People get it in their heads they need a horse, not really understanding what it means to take care of them. They soon find themselves out of their league and fast out of cash. And as is typical, an irresponsible move soon leads to an irresponsible end."

"Will you come back for them?" she asked.

"I'll send a couple of the men out for them tomorrow. They're all right for now. There's plenty for them to graze on out here and not a lot of trouble to get into."

She took a deep breath and scooted back in her seat, a worried scowl upon her brow. He wondered what she was thinking, but wasn't about to ask. The ride thus far had been quite cordial. He didn't want to do anything to ruin it, and something told him prying might.

"How was school?" he ventured, figuring the subject safe.

Back to looking out the side window, his beautiful companion shrugged her shoulder. "It was all right. The first three years went fast enough. Toward the end, it began to drag. There's probably more exciting fields than business. After a while, the classes all seemed the same—dry."

"Glad to have it behind you?"

"Mostly. I made a lot of friends, many who've moved on. I'll miss them."

Mac wondered how many remained and what role they played in her life. He'd actually wondered it many times through the years. He wasn't a fool. A lot of men would be more than willing to fill his brother's shoes.

"So, now what?"

Her chest rose and fell with a deep breath. "Prison," she replied softly, reluctantly.

He cast her reflection a curious glance. Perhaps he'd misheard her over the plane's steady whir. "Prison?"

Their gazes locked in the glass.

She lifted a brow. "What would you call it?"

"Since when did the ranch become a prison? You've always loved it here. Nothing's changed."

"I've changed," she said a bit defensively, though he wasn't entirely sure if she were trying to convince him or trying to convince herself. "I no longer see life through rose-colored glasses. I now prefer the panoramic view, the one that captures the barren miles working as bars."

"Ah, yeah." He recognized the words for what they were—a parroting. "Now, that sounds like Patsy. You always loved the vast land, Grace. In fact, I remember you more than once referring to it as freedom. The barren miles were *her* bars not yours, and in that respect, the ranch has changed. We now have a plane." He patted the control wheel. "With wings, those miles become minutes. We're now no more than an hour from two major hospitals and forty minutes from shopping. That's something you should tell your grandmother."

"He's told her, but it's a little too late. She's reattached to her roots back in Canada. She may come for a visit, but this will never again be her home."

"I hope you're wrong."

"I'm not wrong."

She sat back up in her seat and watched eagerly as they neared the eastern hills, dove into the belly, and headed for the falls.

It truly was a sight to behold—a dry, rugged range cracking in the middle to form a cascade of descending stone ridges that, like a waterwheel, carried water from the hills above down to the rocky surface of a well-shaded chasm.

A great place to swim and escape the Texas heat; his parents had brought him and Garrett here for years. It remained their favorite getaway even to this day.

As the small plane rose out of the gorge to scale the hills, Grace released a heavy sigh. "It hasn't changed at all. It's exactly as I remember it. It will be well worth the ride when I make it."

"Just so you don't make it alone. There's not a lot of danger to run into out here, but it's far enough away from home you can't simply yell for help."

"I'll find someone willing to take the ride. Grandfather says all the old hands are still here Brody, Mick, Tagger, and of course Phil and Jarrod. I know I can talk Jarrod into taking me, probably Tagger as well."

He shot her a glance. "You'd best not be counting on Jarrod to fall all over himself to please you. He's got himself a girl, and Phil says he's crazy about her. I doubt he'll play the role of your lap dog this round."

Her mouth dropped open, but not a sound fell out. Only the drone of the engine filled the space, emphasizing her silence.

"Did you expect him to wait?"

Jarrod had moved to the ranch with his father, Phil, their foreman, when he was twelve. During Grace's many long visits, the two had been nearly inseparable, that is, until she'd started seeing Garrett. If somewhere in the back of her mind she was still thinking of staying, then Jarrod could very well be where she'd next turn her attention.

Mac shifted uncomfortably, telling himself he only cared because Jarrod was his friend.

Her lovely lips closed as her eyes narrowed. "Jarrod and I were friends—only friends. There was never anything else between us. If you remember correctly, there weren't exactly a lot of kids around to play with back then. The only person my age and willing to hang out with me was Jarrod, and that's because he didn't have any choice either. You and Garrett were always off somewhere together or following Grandpa. Our options for friends were few at best. We became pals out of necessity. The friendship grew because we happened to have a lot in common."

"Yeah, all right, if that's the claim you're staking."

Her look of disgust and accompanying sigh said far more than words. She turned to stare back out the window. "I think we should agree not to talk. We're close enough now the silence won't be hard to handle."

Keeping his mouth shut was probably an excellent suggestion, but unfortunately, he felt the need to dig his hole a little deeper. "He was head over heels for you.

The poor bloke wandered around for months like a lost puppy after you left."

"I doubt that. By the time I left, we hardly saw each other."

"He missed you, so did your grandfather. Your leaving was a blow to them both." And for some strange reason, it had come as a blow to Mac as well, which was actually his point.

"I had to leave. They both understood." Shifting her position in her seat, she turned back to glare at him. "Why do you care? I don't see why it should matter to you. You'd wanted me gone for years. I hardly think you're in any position to question my decision or try and throw guilt."

"I never wanted you gone, not exactly. At least…not…well, 'years' is definitely an exaggeration."

Her lovely lips curled into another snarl.

He grimaced. "Oh, come on, Grace. What do you expect? You were a pain in the ass. You were *purposefully* a pain in *my* ass. So, yeah, there were times I wanted you gone."

"Maybe if you hadn't been such a huge *ass* to begin with, I wouldn't have found you such a tempting target."

A point he'd figured out himself many years back.

Aligning the plane back with its original path, he sighed. "You're right. I'm sorry. I should have been kinder."

"And kept your nose out of other people's business."

"I happen to believe my brother *is* my business."

She stared down to the hands she held clenched in her lap. "We're not even supposed to be talking."

"Don't you think it would be better if we actually worked this thing out? You're here at the ranch for two years. It's going to get a little difficult to keep—"

Covering her ears, she began an annoying hum, singing out, "Not listening," for its chorus.

Mac's grip tightened on the controls as he momentarily fantasized about throttling her. *God, the woman can be impossible.*

"He didn't love you, Grace."

The humming got a little louder.

"I know you can hear me."

She repeated the chorus.

Mac gritted his teeth and prayed for patience. One day before she left, he would make her listen, but it would have to be a day he felt a little less like wringing her stubborn neck.

Chapter Three

Storming toward the old, dust-covered truck, Grace began her countdown of her next seven-hundred-and-seventy days in captivity.

One.

She grabbed the truck's door handle and pulled. It didn't budge. A small irritant, considering she'd had every intention of jumping inside and slamming the door closed, making a point as she cut herself off, if only momentarily, from the world of Mac Palmer. She should have known it wouldn't work. The man had always gotten away with seeming larger than any moment.

"I'll get the door," he hollered from behind. Still standing beside the plane retrieving her luggage, he shot her an amused glance before dropping the bags on the ground at his feet. Outlined by the austere land and distant hills, he looked completely at home—rugged and tough, blending with the world around him.

As long as she'd known him, that had always been his truth, and she imagined it was so from the day he was born. The spirit of the land had lived in the Palmer line for years. Buster's Prairie had belonged first to Mac's great-grandfather and had been passed all the way down to Mac and Garrett, interrupted only fleetingly by her own grandfather, who, with no better option, had agreed to hold the land in a sort of trust.

But despite what any papers might say, Grace was certain Mac had never seen the land as anything but his own. Her grandfather used to joke that he wasn't certain between him and Mac who was the teacher and who was the student. Truth be told, it was a little of both.

By the time Mac's father passed, he'd already taught his eldest son all there was to know about ranching on such a rugged land. What Eldon had brought to the table was a great deal of cash, new ideas, and a bucketful of spirit which he'd held on a backburner for too many years.

Buster's Prairie was her grandfather's "dream come true." Her grandmother had often told her that, although Eldon was born in Canada, the stork must have dropped his spirit while flying over Texas. Her grandfather had to come back to make himself whole.

He, like Mac, belonged to the land, and now, as fate would have it, they belonged to each other.

Garrett had always held the dream, but not so much the drive. He'd played second-fiddle with literally no complaint and easy acceptance. Looking back, Grace now realized that persona pretty much defined the love of her early years. He was far too easily led, by Mac, by her. The first real defiance he'd ever shown was the night he'd left her waiting unaware at the Diamond Tail Hotel while he eloped with another.

Grace had just returned to Texas after visiting her parents at their new excavation site in Wales. She'd arrived in Dallas and flown straight to Amarillo where Garrett was supposed to meet her that night at the hotel. From there, they'd planned to elope. But somewhere between her departure from Buster's Prairie and her return from Wales, Garrett had taken her dream and handed it to another.

It still hurt to this day—the betrayal. Whether he'd loved her or not, he should have had the decency to explain, to tell her himself, but instead, he'd sent his big brother, a man who would never cower from a job that needed to be done.

Not that Mac had seemed particularly burdened by the task. He'd never wanted their marriage. He'd never cared for her—maybe because she'd been such a pest in her younger years, or maybe because he saw her as a threat. Perhaps he'd feared if she and Garrett married, her grandfather might be tempted to see the ranch fell into the hands of the younger brother.

It would never have happened. Her grandfather had made it very clear through the years which Palmer he felt worthy. But risk to his precious ranch was something Mac would always take quite seriously.

The slamming of the plane's door snapped Grace out of her musings. Once again, she tried the handle.

Nothing.

Looking back over her shoulder, she caught him slinging her purse across his shoulder as he leaned down to pick back up the bags. It was an amusing sight. She couldn't help but laugh at the muscular man headed her way with a pebbled leather, mahogany purse across his shoulder and dancing flamingos dangling from his hand.

"Not a word," he threatened, dumping the bags into the truck's bed before heading her way.

She gave the door one last try. Still it refused to budge despite the lock showing up. "What's wrong with the door?"

Stepping up behind her, he reached around and

took hold of the handle, yanking the door open with one sure pull. "She's a lot like you. Temperamental. It's her way or no way."

With his cheek so close to hers and his warmth close enough to feel even beyond the heat of the Texas sun, Grace momentarily lost her sense of direction, her mind being thrown unexpectedly back in time, back to that evening at the Diamond Tail when the heat of battle had turned so easily into the heat of desire.

For a split second, she considered leaning back into him. It proved a startling thought. "Bite me," she snapped, pushing past his arm to crawl into the cab.

Mac's laughter drifted to the small space as he pushed the door closed. The nerves along her spine twitched as she squeezed her fingers angrily, digging into the beaten leather seat, hoping to find an anchor for her quickly rising temper. The man didn't even have to try to get on her nerves; he'd been sitting on them so long he had a reserved seat.

Peering into the rearview mirror, she watched as he strolled leisurely around the truck to the driver's side, taking his seat as though he hadn't a clue of her anger. He looked…smug.

She squeezed a little harder. He was the only man she'd ever known who could stir in her such a strong desire to physically attack. She glared his way, reminding herself he was bigger, stronger, likely to fight back and not necessarily fair.

He looked her way and flinched. "Seriously, Grace, you have to get over it."

With that said, he pulled her purse out from under his arm. Then, much to her horror, he reached inside and pulled out her passport before tossing her the bag.

What?

She glanced disbelievingly from her purse back to the passport. "Exactly what do you think you're doing?" Reaching across the seat, she grabbed for the little blue paperback, inadvertently landing in his lap as he lifted his rear to push the book into his back pocket.

His chuckle was low, rumbling, far too amused. "Sweetheart, really…here…now?"

Pushing against his undeniably impressive thighs, she made her way back up to sitting. "No, not here, not now, not *ever*. Give me back my passport."

His reply was a pleased grin.

Turning the keys already dangling from the transmission, he brought the old pickup to life. "It's merely a little assurance you pay before departing."

"Whether or not I pay is none of your business. Now, give me back my passport."

Ignoring her completely, he tossed the truck into drive and headed down the long path to the ranch.

Her temper seethed. "You're every bit the pompous ass I remember, walking around as though everyone else's business somehow equates to yours."

"I care about your grandfather. Like it or not, I'm not going to let you take advantage of him. He deserves better."

"I care about him, too, but we both know there are plenty of other ways I could repay him. This is simply his way of gaining control over me and over my grandmother." Picking up her purse, she snapped closed the opening and tucked the bag safely under her arm.

He eyed the purse and sighed. No doubt recognizing her actions for what they were—a pitiful attempt to gain back some control.

"It was the deal you made, Grace. Take it like a grownup and pay up."

"I would have made a deal with the devil that day to get away from this place."

"To get away from this place…or to get away from me?"

She hesitated, though she knew the answer well. "Both."

Chapter Four

Mac knew it all along. Why it bothered him to hear it from Grace's lips, he wasn't sure, but it did. Garrett may have broken her heart, but *he* was the one she was running from.

How many times had he gone to call her and not?

Countless.

The truth was always there in the back of his mind. She wanted nothing to do with him. She hated him. The spark that had flared between them at the hotel that night had been no more than a fluke. She'd been lost and needed an anchor, and he looked far too much like his brother.

As for him and his response...that was a bit harder to explain.

Sure, Grace was a beautiful woman. A man would have to be blind not to see it, but the idea of the two of them together was new to him that night. He definitely hadn't gone there for that. His plan had been to break the news of Garrett's elopement as easy as possible, and hopefully help her see reason before returning to the ranch and her grandparents—her grandparents who had yet to be told.

If he'd have had any idea how things would end up, he never would have gone. Although, he had to admit, it definitely proved interesting.

The truck bounced over a rut, pulling his attention

back to the here and now. Mac shot Grace a quick glance, but she was looking away, lost in her own thoughts or memories. Leaning forward, he turned on the radio, hoping music would fill the silent gap which suddenly seemed to sit so loud between them.

Topping the hill, the ranch came into full view—its own mini-society made up of a sprawling two-story ranch house, guesthouse, foreman's house, two bunkhouses, a shop, two barns, two large storage sheds, and a newly built stable. Adorned with numerous trees planted throughout the years to provide much needed shading, it had always struck him as a beautiful sight, life at its finest. No matter where he went, how long or how far away, it always felt wonderful coming home to where he was born and raised.

Warm and inviting, its well-manicured lawns housed a good-sized arena, and far to the right of the arena, away from the living quarters, lay an impressive coral complete with a large gathering pen, a round crowd pen, and alley with solid sides, well-kept stalls, and diagonal pens for easy sorting—just one of several great ideas Eldon had brought with him to the ranch.

It was a home any man would be proud of—Mac certainly was.

Grace had once loved the ranch no less than he. *"It's the most beautiful place on Earth,"* she used to say quite regularly and sometimes while running through the yards, spreading her arms as though embracing it all. She'd truly been an adorable little character; although, he could remember at the time calling her odd.

Wondering if any of her youthful passion for the land had survived, he snuck another peek in her direction. But instead of admiring the large sprawl ahead of them, she was eyeing something on the floorboard.

She leaned down to pick it up as Mac returned his attention to the road. Most likely she'd found a knob or some other gadget knocked loose from the dashboard. The truck had seen better days, but for some reason, Eldon was reluctant to declare its retirement.

A soft rattle played just below the bass on the stereo.

On a side glance, he saw Grace sitting back up, holding tight to Ellie's teething ring. It must have rolled out from under the seat when he'd hit the last rut.

Holding it up in the air, she tossed him an impish grin. "Are your wisdom teeth still trying to come in?"

He couldn't help himself and grinned. "Stick your finger in my mouth and find out."

Grace dropped the ring on the seat between them. "Did you marry her?"

Of course her mind would jump to that conclusion. The woman couldn't think any less of him if she tried.

"Marry Ellie?" he asked, pulling his brows in mock confusion. "No, she's a little young for me, not to mention my niece."

Silence filled the cab. Another quick glance her way told him she'd made the right connection. It also told him something else—she hadn't been told.

Had Eldon shared nothing?

"You didn't know?"

She swallowed, looking down at her hands. "No."

A familiar heaviness fell around his heart. He'd felt the same thing that night at the hotel, when, overcome with sadness, she'd let down the guard she'd always held around him and simply fallen apart.

Of course, it hadn't lasted long. She'd recovered fairly quickly and gone straight for the attack. He wondered if he wasn't about to see a repeat performance, but instead, she merely sighed and picked up the ring again.

Mac went back to watching the road. She had to find out sometime. He imagined now was as good a time as any, though, he really wished it could have been someone else that broke the news to her this time.

"How old is she?" Her voice was surprisingly calm.

"Nearly a year. She's really very sweet." He adored Ellie. She'd won his heart the moment she'd wrapped her little fingers around his one.

"Do they…?" She hesitated, took a deep breath, and then continued, "Do they live nearby?"

"They're living with Jackie's family at their ranch outside of Wichita. Garrett's working for Leo, her father, but I imagine he'll be taking over the running of the place in the next year or so."

"Is that right?"

He shot her another glance. "I'm guessing. Leo's been threatening to retire for some time. But this last year, he's actually handed over most of the managing to Garrett."

She moistened her lips with the tip of her tongue, casting him a sideways glance. "That must make you very happy. Your little brother's set for life, and you didn't even have to surrender a piece of Buster's Prairie. Congratulations. Job well done."

Ouch! And there it was, bare and out in the open, Grace Wade's lower-than-low opinion of him.

Gritting his teeth, Mac took a firm grip on the wheel and looked back to the road. "It has nothing to do with me. It never did."

"It has everything to do with you—your wishes, your likes, your dislikes. He idolized you, and you played him like a puppet."

"He didn't love you, Grace, not enough."

"Of course he didn't. He wasn't allowed to." She tossed the rattle back on the seat. "You should have let me go home, Mac. I don't belong here."

"And what about your promise to your grandfather? He lived up to his end. Don't you think you ought to live up to yours?"

"I'll pay him back every dime."

"It's not your money he wants. It's not the deal you made."

And that was a truth she couldn't argue, so he was hardly surprised when she didn't bother to try.

He gave her another glance out of the corner of his eye. "Give it a chance, Grace. Worst case scenario— you hate it and ask for an early release. Then you can leave guilt and obligation free. No more Buster's Prairie. No more Palmer brothers."

Turning away to look out her dust-covered window, she released a heavy sigh. "I'm here, aren't I?"

"That's not the same as giving it a chance."

Her shoulders lifted and fell with another deep breath. "You don't get it, do you, Palmer? I already gave it a chance. I gave it everything I had." Her voice was heavy—dejected, resigned.

With her head turned from him and no kind of reflection offered by the glass, he couldn't see her expression. But the picture for him was still very clear.

The ranch, for her, now meant nothing but pain.

As they passed the tall, log gateway introducing Buster's Prairie, Grace watched the ranch-style dwelling come clearly into view. Still immaculately kept and tastefully landscaped, not a lot had changed outside of the scene in front of it. Since when did her grandfather ever wait anxiously?

"Is that really him?" The tall but slightly frail looking man shaded his eyes from the glare of the sun. In all her many musings through the years, she'd never once considered any changes that might befall the unbreakable Eldon Wade. But standing on the veranda at the top of the stairs was a man she may have passed in a crowd. "What's happened to him?"

"He's seventy-four, Grace. Age is able to catch up a little faster in the later years."

"I never saw him as anything but strong." She scooted closer to the windshield.

"He is strong, but he's also human."

Mac followed the curve of the drive to stop right at the bottom of the veranda's steps. The truck rattled and lurched slightly forward as he shifted it into park. He turned the key and the engine sputtered off.

Patting the dash, he sighed. "Everything and everyone ages." He turned to face her, his expression regretful. "Time shows mercy to no one, not even those who would choose to defy it."

Grace stared past him, out the driver's-side window, and toward the most invincible man she'd ever known. He'd been many things to her through the years—a father, a teacher, and often times her biggest critic. She'd always loved him without question, but she'd always felt a little intimidated by him as well. He was frank, rough, and far too often bitterly direct with his words.

The last word she'd use to describe the man awaiting her now was intimidating. He looked eager, warm, and maybe even—it seemed a ridiculous thought, but came all the same—cuddly.

Hanging onto the stair's railing, her grandfather made his way down to the truck. An unexpected surge of affection ran through her. She reached for the handle and expecting the door to be stubborn both ways, gave a mighty shove. Much to her surprise, the door gave without hesitation, flying wide open. There was no stopping it. Down she went, face first, dignity sailing.

As she groped the dirt and spat out its offering, she heard snickering behind her. Turning, she found Mac leaned across the truck's seat, staring down out the passenger door to where she lay.

"You all right?" he asked, his show of concern seeming a tad artificial on the tail of his laughter.

"Dandy," she grumbled, moving to her knees and then onto her feet. She brushed off the dirt and straightened her skirt.

"Grace?" Her grandfather now stood to the side of the door.

There was the adorable *gramps* she'd always dreamt of—sweet, caring, warm.

He scowled. "I take it charm school wasn't part of the programming at that fancy-prancy college I paid for."

And this is the grandfather I got.

"Hi, Grandpa." She wrapped her arms around him.

He held her tighter than she'd expected and a little longer as well.

"I've missed you, Grace Elizabeth. I'm glad to have you home."

And that would easily classify as the biggest show of affection she'd ever received from the man.

"I love you, too, Grandpa." She kissed his much-more-wrinkled-than-four-years-ago cheek. He'd grown old while she was away, running into a reality she would have sworn he'd find a way to bypass.

"How was the trip?" he asked as he led her back up the stairs toward the veranda.

"Long. I'm beat. Hope you won't mind my settling in with a nap before dinner?"

"Not at all, though I should tell you, Jenny's made us a delicious roast beef with baked potatoes and slow-grilled vegetables. It's one of her best, much better warm than cold."

Jenny, Mac's mother, was a notoriously superb cook. As they made their way up the steps, the mouth-watering aromas drifted from the house to greet her.

"Mmm," she murmured, breathing it in. "It does smell good. Is Jenny here?"

"Was. Her and Doc had to head over to the Ballinger's to help deliver a foal in trouble, then they're heading to Dallas for some kind of veterinarian shindig, and after that, they're off to see Doc's daughter in Fort Worth. They won't be home for better than two weeks."

"They live here on the ranch?"

"Where else?"

"I don't know. I guess I'd assumed she'd moved with him into the city."

"No. It made much better sense for him to move out here. Now, we have our own private veterinarian right here on the ranch. It's an idea I wish I'd have thought of years ago." He stopped at the top of the steps, spreading out his arms. "So, what do you think?"

"Of the veranda?"

"Yes."

The porch swept the entire length of the house. Its front was decorated on one side by a long, picnic-style table covered with an intricately embroidered white tablecloth and topped by a basket filled full of a variety of fruits she knew to be for the ranch hands. It was a quaint tradition her grandmother had started, and one Grace was shocked to see her grandfather had kept. Simple folding chairs sat ready, but tucked in at its sides. A couple pieces of wrought iron décor tactfully graced the walls.

On the opposite side of the veranda was an attractive arrangement of wicker seats decorated with white and green cushions—new to the porch but still similar to those which had been there before. In its middle, hung the same wooden porch swing that had held her for years. Additional iron artwork sat scattered throughout.

"The place looks wonderful, Grandpa. You've done a great job."

Smiling as though immensely pleased, he nodded as he looked around. "Be sure to tell your grandmother. The woman never credits me with a thing but disaster, but this she'd be pleased with. It was always her special getaway."

Oh, dear heavens! Mac was right.

Why hadn't she seen it? Her grandfather *was* still very much in love with her grandmother.

"Grandma is always telling me what a remarkable eye you have for detail." Of course, it was always followed up by, *"Too bad he couldn't show that much attention to our marriage."* But that was a piece Grace felt no need to share.

Her grandfather continued on to the door. "How is she, Grace? Is she happy?" Holding open the screen with the heel of his boot, he pushed open the front door.

Stepping in, she gave the question serious consideration, not entirely certain what answer her grandfather sought. Her grandmother had seemed very happy the first few months in Vancouver. Of course, back then, she'd still been referring to the excursion as a lengthy vacation, believing at the time she'd be returning to Buster's Prairie.

It had struck Grace after a while that Grandma should have returned, but when she'd asked her about it, her grandmother seemed reluctant to discuss the topic. Finally one day, she came right out and said her marriage was over.

By that time, it had come as little surprise.

The following years had all been a bit of a blur. School had kept Grace more than busy. Her relationship with her grandmother, while they were still plenty close, had become less hands-on. They covered the basics and lived their lives side by side, but late-night conversations were replaced with late nights at the library, and weekend outings were replaced with weekend study groups.

There was a period her grandmother had seemed somewhat down. But with Grace's encouragement, she'd joined a local church group and met several new friends who seemed to lift her spirits and fill in the blank space Grace had once filled.

So, why she now found her grandfather's question

so difficult to answer, she wasn't exactly sure.

"I believe she's content," she finally said, noting from the foyer the home's interior looked very much the same. "Have you never asked her?"

Gramps shut the door behind him and turned her way. "Pulling answers from that woman is like pulling teeth from a wild boar. I quit bothering to ask three years back. Are you sure you wouldn't like something to eat before hitting the sack?"

"No." Exhaustion called her to sleep. "I'll enjoy my meal much better when I can keep my lids open to see it. Is Jenny now cooking for you all the time?"

"No, hardly ever. She's too busy helping Doc and fussing over her new grandbaby."

Her new grandbaby.

Grace panicked. "Does that mean Garrett and his wife are here often?"

"They drop in now and again. Jenny spends a lot of free time at their place, and occasionally, she'll bring their little critter back here for a day, never longer though. The little one's momma gets too antsy."

The front door opened, and Mac stepped in, dropping her bags just inside the door. "That's it. I'll check with the hands then be back for supper."

Tilting his head as though the new angle might give him a different view, her grandfather eyed the luggage suspiciously. "Flamingos?"

Mac grinned. "My thoughts exactly."

Gramps blinked and shook his head. "Thanks, Mac. I appreciate your picking up Grace."

Bright blue eyes shined with something akin to mockery as Mac lifted his gaze and looked in her direction. "No problem," he said before ducking back outside.

The muscles around Grace's heart squeezed tight around her suddenly fluttering organ. The man, his smile, his sexy, yet completely annoying, confidence—they all had a way of sneaking up on her and triggering a response they had no right activating. The rogue was undeserving.

Stupid genetics.

"Mac and I share the cooking," her grandfather continued as he turned back her way.

Share the cooking? Her misbehaving heart froze and her stomach knotted. He couldn't possibly mean—

"Neither one of us is much in the kitchen. I was kind of…" He paused as he caught her mortified expression. "Uh, hoping you'd take over. Grace, is something wrong?"

"Grandpa, is Mac living here?" She pointed to the floor beneath her feet. "In *this* house?"

"Well, of course, where did you think he was staying?"

"Ah…in the guesthouse, where he's always lived."

"He hasn't always lived in the guesthouse, Grace. This was his house first, and as it will be again, I figured he may as well get comfortable in it. Besides, Jenny and Doc now live in the guesthouse. He can't very well stay there. They're newlyweds, and she's his mother. It would be too uncomfortable."

Uncomfortable. Yeah, she got that and didn't want it either. "So, have him move into one of the bunkhouses."

"Nonsense. There's plenty of room here. You'll see it yourself. It will get plenty lonesome here in this monster even with the three of us."

"Lonesome is underrated."

Gramps chuckled. "No, darlin', it's not. Take it from an old man who's come to know. Come on." He grabbed her luggage and turned toward the stairway. "I'll show you to your room. Same one as before. Two down from mine and your grandmother's."

"Here, Grandpa, let me grab—"

It was pointless. He was already gone, packing her bags as though he hadn't aged a day.

Realizing any further argument was futile, she followed him up the stairs. She was beyond tired, both physically and mentally.

How can things possibly get any worse? Two years seemed an impossibly long time to share a house with someone she loathed as much as she did Mac Palmer, especially when the advantage wouldn't be hers. She'd literally be living in a throng of his admirers. Everyone at Buster's Prairie believed the man some kind of irreproachable god. There'd be no one to commiserate with, not even Jarrod, who never had understood her dislike for the man.

She was doomed, and that wasn't even the worst of it. Two years was more than enough time to incorporate numerous "occasional visits" from the younger Palmer brother and his replacement-player bride.

Great. Just fantastic.

It was exactly what she didn't need—the reenactment of her childhood dream played out right in front of her by the family that should have been hers.

"This is it." He stopped outside her door and dropping her luggage. Turning back around and leaning forward, he kissed her forehead. "Have a good nap. Come down whenever you're ready."

"Thanks, Grandpa."

"I'll give your grandmother a call. Let her know you made it here all right."

She smiled. "I know she'd appreciate it."

Nodding, he seemed perhaps a bit choked up. "I meant what I said, Gracie. It's nice to have you home. Things just haven't been the same with you and your grandmother gone."

For Eldon Wade to make such a confession, he really had to have been lonely.

Once again, emotion overtook her, and she wrapped her arms around him. "It's good to be home, Grandpa." And surprisingly, at that moment, she really meant it.

Chapter Five

Mac paused outside the kitchen entry.

"She's already sleeping," Eldon was saying, no doubt talking with Patsy, "but I knew you'd be waiting for her call, and I didn't want you to worry."

Why the man didn't come right out and ask her to come home, he would never understand. Maybe Grace was right, maybe Patsy had already cut the strings. Either way, if the old man would ask, at least he'd know and could go on with his life. Or maybe not. Maybe not knowing was better at seventy-four years old.

"No, don't trouble yourself unless you're looking to get away. She'll be fine. I'm capable of looking after her."

Ouch. Mac cringed. Had Eldon really just turned down an offer from Patsy to come home? The man couldn't possibly be that daft, could he?

"Oh, all right. Yes, I'll tell her. Take care," Eldon said, ending the conversation.

He was staring at the phone when Mac walked into the room. "Patsy?"

His old friend glanced up, seemingly surprised to find him standing there. "Hmm? Oh, yes. I was letting her know Grace made it home all right."

"She offered to come out?"

Forming a bridge with his thumb and forefinger, he

placed it between his brows and massaged the area. "She offered. I imagine she thinks I can't take care of her like she would. The woman always has been a coddler."

"Maybe." Mac walked past him to the fridge and took out a soda. "Or maybe she was simply looking for an excuse to come home." Popping the can's lid, he headed back to the table, taking a seat across from his friend.

The old man eyed him curiously. "Did Grace say something to that effect?"

"No, but it's certainly a possibility."

Eldon scowled. "If she wants to come home, she should say so."

Mac chuckled and shook his head, remembering an earlier conversation with Grace. "How did the two stubborn goats decide who'd cross the road first?"

"What?"

"The correct response is, 'How?'"

The scowl grew deeper before lightening with understanding. "Oh, how?"

"They didn't. They're still standing on the wrong side refusing to be first."

Eldon stared blankly at him a moment then grinned. "She's a stubborn woman, all right. I imagine the two of us together could hold a deadlock for years."

"I imagine."

"I love her."

"I know," Mac said before taking a long swig from the can.

Tapping his fingers against the phone, Eldon pursed his lips and gave it more thought. "I never wanted her to leave, but I was too proud to say so.

Thought she'd turn tail and head back without any offerings." Chuckling, he shook his head and tapped the phone again. "Pride has its place, but it's rarely beside a stubborn old fool."

Mac's thoughts instantly fell back to his past dealings with Grace. "Doesn't matter the age, pride and foolish never partner well."

The "old fool" stared back at the phone. "I don't want to waste any more time living without her."

"Then don't."

"What if she says no?"

"Don't make it a question." He looked up to the ceiling and nodded, indicating the floor above where one beautiful but painfully stubborn woman slept. "That granddaughter of yours is definitely a handful. It's common sense, not weakness, to accept help."

A bright smile lit the older man's face. "I like the way you think, Mr. Palmer."

Picking up his can, Mac rose to his feet and patted Eldon's shoulder on his way out of the room. "Go get her, tiger," he encouraged.

"Good advice, son. I believe I'll offer you the same."

Pausing only momentarily before heading out into the foyer, Mac wondered if he'd heard the old man correctly. Certainly not. Eldon hadn't a clue what all had transpired between him and Grace. And *no one* knew how he felt about her. Even he wasn't entirely clear on that one. The woman made him crazy. No one saw clearly through crazy.

Walking straight through the foyer and out the front door, he stopped at the top of the veranda steps to look out over the ranch.

He loved the view and everything it came with—the amazing array of orange that splashed nearly every night in varying patterns across the horizon, the familiar shadows that fell slowly across the grounds, offering relief from the day's heat, the balls of dust rising from the arena along with the hoots and hollers of his men as they spent their last few hours trying to ride two notoriously temperamental bulls. Though it meant the world to him, still, Grace was wrong. He'd never begrudge his brother any of it. If things had turned out differently and Garrett had married Grace, he'd have worked beside his brother gladly, sharing the dream of their father and grandfathers without an ounce of resentment.

He hadn't questioned Garrett's feelings for Grace because he wanted the land, he'd questioned his brother's feelings because he'd come to him with doubts. Mac did what any good brother would do—he encouraged his little brother to go slow and be leery, coached him to keep his mind open and not settle down too young. At no time had he ever actually forbidden anything. He'd simply given guidance—guidance he'd hoped would stay between the two of them.

Unfortunately, it hadn't.

Though he'd been careful to make sure Grace was never anywhere near, it soon became obvious his brother had shared with her some of what he'd said. So, when things got worse between the two of them, Grace blamed him for it all—Garrett's uncertainties, his withdrawal, and in the end, his betrayal.

In truth, Mac knew he could be to blame. It wasn't chance that had introduced Jackie to Garrett. It was him, and yes, he'd known exactly what it was he was doing.

A roar of cheers rang from the arena. Shaking off his troubled thoughts, Mac headed that way.

"Ah, pull your head in, braggart," Phil Donner yelled to Lance Poe, the newest hand to have joined their crew and therefore, the target of much harassment. "If your boot hadn't been stuck in the rope, you'd have been ducking under the fencepost," the foreman added.

"Bugger off, Donner," hollered the young cowboy, the grin on his face saying no real offense had been taken.

Leaning in against the fence beside Phil, a well-seasoned cowboy by any man's account, Mac pushed back his hat and nodded toward their youngest recruit. "Had a good run, I take it?"

The man nodded, his chest rising and falling with a silent chuckle. "That kid can ride like nothing I've ever seen. Youngin's these days don't have the sense to be scared of nothing. It's their advantage as well as their weakness."

"You'll keep an eye on him?"

"I keep an eye on all of 'em, boss, especially that youngin' of mine. Not that there's much need. We've got a good crew here. It pays to hire those with the knowhow and background. Rookies might be cheap, but you definitely get what you pay for."

"That's exactly what my father always said, and why I hire like I do. A ranch this size can't run on training wheels."

Looking across to the chutes, he spotted Jarrod positioning himself over the top of the small bucking stall. Behind him, coming up through the chute, was an unhappy looking bull by the name of Last Ride.

Mac laughed. "That cowboy's determined."

"Care to place a wager?" Phil asked with a sheepish glance his way.

"Mmm, no. I've emptied too much of my pocket into your hands already. My judgment's obviously off. But tell me what you're thinking."

"I'm thinking it's his head and not the bull that's been beating him. Once he gets it in his head he can ride it, he'll hold the eight."

Mac sighed. "Self-doubt's a hard thing to beat."

"That it is," the foreman said, his grin spreading wider across his rugged face. "How about you? Thinking about giving it a go?"

"No." He ignored his friend's taunting grin, instead focusing in on the man's son currently waiting anxiously atop the chute. "And before you say a word, it's not about self-doubt, it's about intelligence. I know better. I don't question whether or not I can ride him. I can, but not every time. It's a gamble, and tonight, I'm simply not in the mood."

"Sounds like an excuse."

The taunt in Grace's voice sent an odd kind of tingle straight down his back. He wasn't entirely sure if he'd been slammed or flirted with.

Turning his head to follow her arrival through to the fence, he almost wished he hadn't. Trouble or not, the woman was an eyeful hard not to react to.

Now dressed in form-flattering jeans and a simple but becoming emerald blouse, she was a vision if ever there was one. Add to that the sexy slant of her tan cowboy hat, which accentuated well the golden highlights of her touch-me-please long hair, and it was utterly impossible to do anything but gawk.

"Well, looky here, boys," Phil hollered from behind him. "The prettiest lady in all of Oz has returned to add a little class to this sorrowful bunch."

"Woowee," Mick Colton yelled from across the arena where he stood waiting to open the chute's door. "Now there's a sight for sore eyes."

"Certainly a far cry prettier than any of your ugly mugs," Jarrod added, waving across to Grace.

Lance Poe, still heading across the arena their way, stopped dead in his tracks to stare, by all appearances having momentarily lost consciousness.

"You're gonna catch flies with that trap set so wide," Phil yelled to the captivated ranch hand.

Snapping out of his trance, Lance merely smiled and took off his hat, nodding Grace's direction. "Miss."

She nodded back. "Nice ride, cowboy. Caught it from my window."

His smile grew, disappearing only a second as he ducked between fence-posts, moving out of the arena into the spectator's corner where they all stood.

"Thought you were sleeping," Mac said, for some reason annoyed by all the attention she was collecting.

She moistened her lips then nodded to the arena. "I heard the fun and couldn't resist." Holding on to the fence post, she leaned back and looked around him. "Hey, Phil, how've you been?"

"You know me, mean and ornery. Just ask the crew."

Her breathtaking smile suggested she knew better. "Still got 'em snowed, do ya?"

"It's all about image, sweetheart."

"She doesn't like being called sweetheart," Mac said, watching their friendly exchange with no small degree of irritation. The woman could actually be charming when she wanted to be.

"Phil can call me sweetheart if he wants to," she corrected then stood back straight, only to lean forward across the fence. "Come on, Jarrod," she cheered across the arena. "You can do it, buddy!"

Every nerve Mac knew and then some prickled with a rambunctious mix of irritation, envy, and awareness. How was he going to make it through the next two years? The woman had him dancing on his nerves after only one short day.

The sound of wood being battered rang from the other side of the arena. Through the slits in the bucking chute's boards, the bull's dark, stormy eyes glared.

"That's a nasty looking bull," Grace noted with a grimace.

"Last Ride," Lance said, having joined them at the fence. He offered her his hand. "And I'm Lance Poe."

"Grace Wade. Nice to meet you." She accepted his handshake as she nodded back toward the chutes. "So, is the bull as bad as he looks?"

"I'd say so. Brody and I are the only ones who've ever stayed with him for the count, and to date, that's only once each."

"You don't say?" She turned Mac's direction, pushing back her hat and studying him with a barely held grin. "The great Mac Palmer hasn't yet stayed the count?"

His lip twitched with irritation as the muscles along his back and shoulders tensed. "First rule of the arena, Grace—he who opens his mouth, gets the next ride."

Moistening her lovely lips with the tip of her tongue, she made no effort to hide her amusement.

"Would watching me break my neck help heal your wounded pride?"

Man, she's good at placing her knives.

Phil grimaced as he reached to the back of his neck and rubbed. "I swear, Grace, I've never met a woman more apt to wear red into the center of a bull ring."

Stunning blue eyes shined with deviltry. "Not in one I couldn't handle."

And if that wasn't a battle cry, Mac didn't know what was. Grace Wade might look like her mother, but there was a whole lot of her grandfather sitting inside her soul.

"Here he goes," Phil said, directing their attention back to the chute just as its door was pulled open.

Last Ride stormed from his enclosure, releasing his fury with a wild bolt into the air.

With his free hand held high, Jarrod managed the flight by following the twist of the bull and directing his own fall in line with his host's.

"That's it, Jarrod!" Mac found himself instantly drawn into the ride.

The bull reared then bucked again, hitting a height that seemed impossible for the size of the beast.

His hand holding firm to the rope, Jarrod kept claim to his seat even as his backside flew into the air.

"Stick with him," Phil hollered from Mac's right.

"Ride him, cowboy," Grace yelled at his left.

All along the fence, friends and co-workers aligned, safe on the ground but nonetheless taking what was proving to be an incredible ride.

Last Ride laid it on thick—throwing his full force into a chaotic arrangement of twists and turns. But the cowboy was in it for the long haul, determination holding his seat as wits kept track of his direction.

"Time," Mick called from his post atop the chute a second before Jarrod was given a see-you-later heave from the bull.

Jumping from his seat atop the pen to the floor of the arena, Mick hit the ground nearly in unison with Jarrod. Only the young cowboy had met the earth on his belly.

Brody and Tagger were already there, vying for Last Ride's interest before his sights got centered on his most recently departed. In the end, Brody won the brute's attention, leading him out of the arena and into the exiting chute.

Grace and Lance scaled the fence together, both heading for the cowboy hobbling their way with a broad smile plastered across his face.

Mac, along with one very proud foreman, soon followed.

Lance made it to his friend first, exchanging a palm to backhand slap of celebration and a shared round of congratulations.

But Jarrod soon looked around his buddy in search of Grace. "There's my good luck charm. Where have you been?" he asked, spreading out his arms to welcome her in.

She moved to his embrace without hesitation, squealing with delight as he lifted her off the ground and swung her around.

An unfamiliar burning sensation flared deep in Mac's chest.

Phil snorted at his side. "Got it bad, do you, boss?"

Until then, Mac hadn't even realized he was glaring. "I don't know what you're talking about."

"Yeah, all right, I'll play it your way." Phil slapped him on the back then leaned in closer. "But for the record, she's not completely immune. I've known that little lady long enough to read her bad behavior. She might not want to be, but she's attracted to you."

"Maybe it's your judgment that's off," Mac said, still eyeing resentfully the all-too-happy group in front of him. "She hates me. And when I say hates, I mean despises."

"Giving you a little of your own, is she?"

He shot his friend an incredulous stare. "I never hated Grace."

"She annoyed you. Everyone saw it but her." Glancing in her direction, he shook his head and sighed. "Cute little thing, she followed you like an old hound. Always knew one day the tables would turn. Of course, I never figured it would take you so long."

"You drop bullshit better than these bulls," Mac accused before turning his attention back to Jarrod and heading his way.

Phil's laughter rumbled at his heels.

****

The mouth-watering smell of a perfectly-cooked roast beef met Grace the moment she walked inside the door. She stopped and smiled, taking in a deep breath of the aroma. The emptiness of her stomach immediately jabbed against her ribs, urging her to hurry.

Real food. There was nothing like it.

The zealous smile faded somewhat as she stepped into the kitchen and found Mac reaching into the microwave above the stove, pulling out his plate. Tall, broad shoulders, lean hips and long, muscular legs—the sight hit her with one mind-blowing punch of appreciation. The man might be a pain in her caboose, but he was also one impressive piece of incredible male.

Turning with the heaping plate steaming in front of him, he spotted her and stopped. "I figured you'd eaten."

"Not yet," she said, drawn out of her appreciative daze and lulled back to the purpose of her journey by the delicious looking cuisine sitting piled upon his plate. "Leave me any?"

He looked to his feast and then back to the empty platters sitting beside the sink. "Hold on." He stepped back to the counter and set down his plate before reaching into the cupboard and pulling out another.

She'd have stopped him there and then and insisted she'd make something else, but the smell of *good* had hit her hard with too sweet a promise. Sacrifice was out of the question. She hadn't eaten a decent meal in going on seventy-two hours. Having gotten a whiff of quality, her palate now refused to suffer.

After splitting his pile equally, Mac pulled out another set of utensils and headed for the table.

Though she would have loved to have taken his offering and run, it seemed rude at that point not to join him, so she chose the seat in front of her. "Thanks," she said as he laid down her plate.

"You're welcome. Glad you caught me before it was all gone."

Eying the two still plenty-full plates, she vowed to remember never again to miss a meal. It was something she hadn't until now thought of—living with two men was going to be quite different from living with only one other woman.

They ate in silence all the way through their meals, Mac finishing first then leaning languidly back in his seat. Closing his eyes, he continued to stretch.

Long, lean muscles rippled beneath light denim as the chair tilted back to accommodate the elongation of his frame. Solid male lay momentarily out on full display. Yeah, she took advantage and stole a glimpse…or two.

His eyes opened, and she instantly diverted hers to her plate.

All four of the chair's legs landed back on the floor. "We usually share kitchen duty," he said, breaking the silence.

Chewing her last piece of beef, she merely nodded.

"Of course, if you're anything like your grandmother in the kitchen, we could look into shifting the split to your favor."

Taking a moment to finish chewing and then swallow her food, she watched his hopeful expression with an odd mix of both mirth and annoyance. Of course, everything the man did managed to, in one degree or another, annoy her.

"My favor?"

His smile proved roughish. "It can all be yours if you like."

"Good try," she awarded him, lifting one of the paper napkins from the holder sitting at the table's center.

"Not a cook?" One very sexy brow rose with surprise, or maybe it was challenge.

Wiping her hands and mouth, she then dropped the napkin to her plate. She fantasized a moment about wiping the smug look off his face with one of her killer dishes, but she was pretty sure that would serve as his win. "I'm a great cook, but it's not my job description."

His brows bumped together atop the bridge of his nose. "You've been given a job description?"

A funny kind of shiver tiptoed across her chest. It seemed extremely unfair that even the man's bad behavior could strike her as sexy. Stilling herself against the urge to touch him, she leaned a little farther back in her chair. "It's not what I was brought here to do, though I don't mind doing my share."

Tilting his head, his brows still pulled, he would have seemed seriously perplexed, but for his eyes that shined with menace. "I'm pretty sure there's not an actual description, and I'm absolutely positive neither Eldon nor I would argue shifting kitchen duty."

He seemed to want it so bad there was no way she was giving it to him, so she opted to ignore him.

"You prepared the meal," she said, grabbing his empty plate and placing it atop hers. "I'll clean up."

"Fair enough." He gathered the utensils and dropped them atop the plates as she rounded up the used napkins.

A few minutes later, she was wrists-deep in suds. She'd assumed he'd leave once she'd graciously taken over, which was actually the point, but instead, he merely scooted his chair angled to the table and sat back to watch her work.

"Feel free to leave," she tossed over her shoulder what definitely was intended as a hint.

"I have something I need to talk to you about." He pushed himself from the chair and walked over to the sink. After grabbing the towel hanging from the counter door in front of her waist, he began drying the platters and plate currently lying on the "cleaned" side of the sink. "I know you're not here to work for me, Grace, but the men here are. I can't have you disrespecting me in front of them."

An irritated set of nerves tiptoed up her spine.

She got the point, and understood it even, but that didn't mean she had to hand it to him nicely. "Let me get this straight." She offered him the next plate. "As long as I disrespect you in private, you're good with it?"

He didn't immediately respond, instead taking the time to thoroughly dry the dish. "Let's just say, I'll tolerate it better."

Rinsing off the silverware, she glanced his way over her shoulder. "You're asking a lot."

"I'm actually not asking at all." Taking the dried plates, he took a step to his right and put them back into the cupboard. Another step back and he held out his hand for the silverware she still held tight in her fist underneath running water.

She could feel the hairs on her nape standing at full alert. He was telling her what she would do, a concept which wasn't sitting well upon her sense of self-righteousness. Grace had years of compiled IOUs she was eager to pay back.

Reaching up past the faucet, he lowered its handle. "Grace?" He nudged his outstretched hand toward the utensils.

She thought about gouging him with them. Up until that point, despite what basically equated to him abducting her, she'd felt as though she'd somehow kept the upper hand. This was, without question, him taking some of that power back. Holding tight to the knives and forks was her own pathetic attempt at holding tight to the reins—reins that were eventually taken from her hands and dried by another.

"Eldon handed over the running of the ranch to me years ago. Buster's Prairie is a large ranch, respect here is a must. I do my part to earn it. I'm sure you understand."

She did, and any further resistance would be childish at best. "Of course," she said, no longer looking his way.

He stood there silently a few seconds longer. For what, she wasn't sure, but whatever it was, he must have determined it unimportant.

"Good night, Grace," he eventually offered. And with that, he was gone—message delivered, point made loud and clear.

Dang, but if he hadn't gone and spoiled all her fun.

****

Terry cloth bathrobe wrapped tightly around her middle and her arms loaded with floral-scented body bath, shampoo, and her favorite conditioner, Grace opened her bedroom door and stepped out into the hall. Across the foyer, the bathroom door was closed. The sound of running water told her someone had beat her to her night's planned oasis.

Rats. Her shoulders dropped forward as she sighed with disappointment.

A quick glance down the hall to Mac's open door tagged him the culprit. Why was she not surprised? She shook her head and scoffed at her own misfortune. At least he seemed like the no-nonsense kind of guy who'd make a shower quick.

Pivoting around, she stepped back into her room.

74

She'd leave the door open and listen for her turn...and, yeah, maybe steal a peek of the half-naked man who'd soon be heading back to his room. He owed her something for her inconvenience, after all.

Dropping her armful of goods onto the bed, she then plopped down right beside them. Back home, she wouldn't have to wait. She'd have the tub all to herself. Her grandmother was an early riser, always taking her showers first thing in the morning. She claimed the steam cleared away her "fog" while the water massaged the "grumble" out of her muscles.

They had a good routine, her and her grandmother.

Her heart ached as a sense of sadness overtook her. She already missed her terribly. It would be a long two years if she couldn't talk her into joining them, at least for a visit, here at the ranch. Her mind wandered back to her earlier conversations with Mac and her grandfather. How had she missed, so completely, the fact that her grandfather's grouchy rumblings were merely his way of saying he missed his wife? She should have known. If she hadn't been so lost in her own self-pity, she would have seen it.

Grace sighed, the slow exhale merging with the sound of the distant waterfall.

Come on, Mac, hurry up.

She'd been looking forward to a long, leisurely bath, bubbles to the rim, soft music playing as she relaxed. Curse Mac's interference. The man should be given a trophy. He was the best at foiling her plans—years ago, her engagement, and then today, her escape. She still couldn't believe it. The man honestly had way too much nerve. First he kidnaps her at the airport. Then, as though that wasn't bad enough, he takes away her passport. What a—

Wait a minute...

Her gleeful squeal bounced around the room, drowning out the sound of the distant waterfall.

My passport!

She jumped from the bed, excitement sending adrenaline rushing through her like a starving dog having gotten whiff of a bone. *Man*, was she ever in need of a bone, and this could be it.

Things had moved mighty fast since they'd arrived back at the ranch. There was a chance he hadn't had time to hide it or that he'd possibly even forgotten he had it. If her luck had changed—and wasn't it about due—maybe, just maybe, she could gain back some of the control she'd lost in the never-ending power-struggle between her and Mac.

Walking back to her door, she checked the hall for the status quo.

Water still running in the bathroom, bedroom door still ajar—it was the golden opportunity she couldn't ignore.

Hurrying down the passage, her heart raced with a mixture of hope and trepidation. It would be better than great to have such a sweet score to dangle over her tormentor's head, but getting caught would be...well, not ideal.

Stopping right outside his room, she shot another look-see toward the bathroom. Coast clear. Tyrant still washing off the day's grime.

Too bad water couldn't send arrogance down a drain, not that his would fit.

Grace snickered and moved inside.

The room was clean for a guy's room, which didn't

really surprise her. The man loved order, everything in its designated place—its place according to Mac.

The second thing that hit her was the familiar scent of male—his scent. She drew a deep breath and glanced at his bed. An unexpected urge to dive straight into the middle startled her back to her mission. She needed to make it quick.

His denim shirt lay tossed across the bed's end, his socks and T-shirt underneath it on the floor, but his pants were nowhere to be seen.

Pursing tight her lips, she clenched her fists at her side. *Rats and double rats!*

She should have guessed he wasn't a robe sort of guy. He was more the drop-your-jeans-outside-the-shower kind of guy, which was going to make things a whole lot trickier. Shoulders slumped, course of action undetermined, she turned back to the hall, and...

A plastic-covered blue book sat upon his dresser.

Now that was just sloppy, almost insulting, but...she'd take it.

Grace darted across the room. Grabbing the book, she slid it inside the robe's inner pocket. She felt like the Grinch, so very pleased and ever-so-slightly devious. Only she wasn't stealing from good little boys and girls. She was taking back stolen goods from a very naughty man. One who'd be returning very soon if the lack of running water was any indication.

Crap!

Her heart skipped a beat. She tensed, tilting her ear a little closer to the door. She didn't hear anyone coming, but that wouldn't be true for long.

She stormed out of his room just as the bathroom door opened and a towel-clad cowboy stepped out.

Grace froze, as did he. Their gazes met, her eyes widening with alarm as his narrowed with suspicion.

Fear shoved her pulse to racing even as her legs stood still. *Okay, this isn't going to end well.* Finally, impulse overrode terror, and she bolted for her room.

But Mac's arms folded around her long before she even made it halfway. Wet yet warm, solid yet soft, sexy yet…well, sexy stood alone—the man was hot, and by the look on his face, apparently steamed.

Faster than she could mark his intent, he had her spun around and headed right back into his room.

The door closed and a lock turned.

"Hey!" She shrugged herself away from his hold then turned back to face him. "Who do you think you are?"

His gaze dropped to her housecoat, his eyes narrowing into two thin slits as he searched for a possible hiding spot. Much to her surprise and horror, he reached right into the outer pocket, the back of his hand bumping against her thigh through the cloth as he searched.

She swatted at the intrusion, playing a bit more offended than she actually was.

He withdrew the hand, his gaze shifting to her eyes. His voice set on no-nonsense, he demanded, "Hand it over."

"What?" Her nerves had her lids batting like a fan on high. She turned her head slightly but never dared look away. "Hand what over?"

He looked to the dresser, snorted, then held out his hand. "Now."

Shifting her body to where the book lay the farthest out of his reach, she took her first stand. "It's mine."

"I don't care." His mesmerizing blues turned almost black.

Grace nibbled at her lip as she sized up the cowboy. Above the towel sat firm and well defined abs, a muscular chest, and broad shoulders that looked no less impressive for the jeans slung nonchalantly over one side. Strength—the man definitely had the advantage.

Yeah, this can only end one way. Unless…

She sniffed, looked away. "Please." This was a battle she'd never win by force, but with wit, she felt she might have something on him.

He hesitated.

It was working. She wanted to laugh. *Guys are so easy.*

She sniffed again. "I can't explain it, but I need it." She looked back his way, lids heavy, timid, the perfect persona of a damsel in distress. She wasn't such a bad actress.

He lifted his hand, rubbing his jaw as he eyed her warily.

Grace sensed victory, and the thrill was exhilarating. "Please," she tried again, this time extending her lip for added effect.

His eyes narrowed again. He lifted the hand higher, dangling his palm directly in front of her chest. "Good try, Grace. Now, hand it over."

Frustration mulled failure inside her head, causing her lips to tremble as she snarled. "You're such an ass."

Amusement flashed in his eyes as its echo lifted his lips. "There's the minx I know and know how to handle. Hand it over, sweetheart…or I'm going in after it."

She gasped, pulling her robe tighter. "It's mine."

"Again, I don't care."

Grace glared her disdain as she clenched her fists around the fabric. She really wanted to slap the arrogance right off his face—a plan instantly vetoed by his sudden look of exasperation.

"One," he started counting.

She huffed and turned around, leaving him to stare at her back. Reaching inside her robe, she pulled out the passport. She'd have to give it back. She hated to do it. In fact, it actually pained her, a real, physical pain, but she saw no way out.

Slowly, she turned back around and stuck her nose in the air. "I'm going to tell my grandfather." She didn't care if it sounded childish, the whole ordeal was absurd.

He grinned. "Knock yourself out. He's right down the hall."

Fury burned with resentment deep inside her chest. He knew her too well. She'd leave her grandfather out of it, especially when she wasn't entirely sure whose side he'd be on.

She fought back the only way she knew how. "You're an ass!"

Mac sighed. "Used. Come on, Grace, can't you come up with anything original?"

Sexy ass was the only alternative that came to mind, and *that* would hardly relay the depth of her aggravation. So, with her head held high above the indignity of it all, she marched her bettered-self right back toward his door, shoving the passport hard into his middle as she passed.

It would have made for an impressive exit had the lock not refused to turn properly. After several failed attempts, she merely slapped the nickel-coated device and glared back at her captor. "What's wrong with the stupid lock?"

He chuckled at her frustration as he reached around her, pulled the door tight against the frame's metal plate, and then effortlessly flipped the lock. "She, too, is a lot like you," he drawled not far from her ear. "A little hard to work...but manageable."

Her gasp was resounding. She'd have given him a good piece of her mind right there and then had her wits been anywhere near her. Unfortunately, they were gone. The feel of his body so close, the warm rush of his breath, and that chest, *oh good grief,* so warm, solid, bare—they'd sent her knees wobbling and her mind running scared.

Finally, she opened the door, but when he refused to take a step back, she was forced to side step to her right and then squeeze herself out. Not exactly the memorable exit she'd been hoping to execute.

Mac couldn't help but grin as he watched Grace scurry down the hall to disappear behind her door. How was it he could find someone who was so gratingly irritating so oddly adorable? With her nose held so high in the air, her lips had been lying at exactly the right angle to...

An odd beat in his chest sent a warning to his senses. *Come on, Mac, don't be an idiot. It's Grace, aka Trouble.*

He shut the door and glanced over to his dresser.

That was stupid—leaving the book out in plain sight. Of course the little imp would have no problem stepping across the boundaries of a simple door. The woman had an arsenal of nerve packaged as outrage, and it was all directed at him.

Walking across to his bed, he dropped the passport onto his nightstand and tossed the jeans he'd had slung over his shoulder on top of the pile already accumulating at the end of his bed.

He'd pick them up tomorrow. Tonight, he was beat.

The towel joined the pile.

The day, an odd mix of excitement, turmoil, and mental warfare, had simply done him in. There was a time he could take Grace's punches without missing a stride. Many times they'd done no more than amuse him. He could actually remember looking forward to her quick-witted, biting repartees, even at times taunted them out of her.

He turned off the bedside lamp then slid underneath the covers. Whatever skill or tolerance he'd had for dealing with her had clearly been lost over the last four years. Her dislike sat a little less comfortably on his conscious. Her jabs dug a little deeper into his pride.

He grinned. At least she hadn't gotten back her passport.

Now, more than ever, he was determined to keep it from her, and it wasn't all about assurance. The woman wasn't the only one with a score to settle. Grace had been going at him for years—purposefully disagreeing with him about everything. And it had started well before her relationship with his brother, so it hadn't all come from that. She'd simply been determined to be a royal pain in his ass and had succeeded quite nicely.

Mac slowly took in and let out a deep breath.

God, she looked hot in that ridiculous robe. Maybe

it was that it begged to be taken off. The thought had definitely crossed his mind a time or two…or the entire time she was with him. When she scooted past him to turn and tuck back out the door, he'd nearly lost it. She'd felt so good against him, he'd thought about grabbing her and pulling her back in.

He grew uncomfortably hard as he imagined what they'd be like together. It was a thought that sent him reeling back in time, back to those final minutes at the hotel. He'd thought about that night often over the years. What was that? Where had it come from—from the heat of an enormous battle to the heat of a desire so strong it had taken over the whole of him? He'd never before and never since felt such a wave of desire.

By her reaction, he'd have to say it had been as powerful for her.

They'd both jumped, literally jumped back away from each other—stunned by the spark their fiery battle had ignited. After that, things had happened in a bit of a blur. She'd scampered around the hotel room collecting her things, babbling undecipherables he was never certain were meant for him. The next thing he knew, she was gone.

Poof.

He'd been left there with a horrendous need, a need so strong it left him unable to follow. And yes, he had wanted to. It had been primal, the desire that raged within him. If she had stayed, regardless of their circumstances, he would have taken her in his arms and made love to her until they were spent.

His brother's fiancée, or so she had been only hours before that. What kind of man did that make him?

He'd wondered then, and he wondered it now—

was that how it would have been between them if it had been him and not his brother who had stolen her heart? Or was it merely a spark forged from the heat of battle? Was it all about the fight?

It was hard not to think about, and he'd thought about it often through the years, the what-ifs continuously playing in his head. What if he'd kissed her? What if she'd kissed him back? What if she hadn't run?

But she had.

In fact, to add insult to injury, the next morning, she confiscated their flight and headed for home, leaving him stranded. By the time he made it back to the ranch, she and Patsy were already gone.

Like they always did, his insides tensed against the memory.

Of course, it was for the best. He knew it was for the best. It wasn't him she had wanted, and he had no desire to play second fiddle, nor did he have any desire to be a means to an end. And he would have always wondered if that was all he was if they had ended up together. Just as he'd always wondered if that was what Garrett was—the answer to her dreams, the perfect fit to the happily-ever-after she'd been building in her head for years—her, the ranch, a family made to fit.

Mac groaned and turned his back to the bedroom door.

As things now stood, if he wanted, he'd have a chance to test the theory.

Based on Grace's own admission, and her rather sad attempt to get back her passport, he was convinced her happily-ever-after no longer included Buster's Prairie. In fact, to sell her on the idea of him, he'd now also have to sell her on the ranch.

Did he want to?

He must be insane, because he was starting to think maybe he did. From the moment she'd stepped from the sky bridge into the terminal and snarled her beautiful lips his way, he hadn't been able to think of anything or anyone else.

Pushing the covers back, he rolled out of bed, grabbed the passport, and hid it under his mattress.

Chapter Six

Closing the ledger, Grace dropped the pencil she'd held poised and ready to strike. There wasn't an error to correct or an item left to add. Just like the equipment logs that held every purchase and repair of machinery, the supply logs that captured everything from fencing supplies to hay, and the health records that had recorded every animal, its every vaccination, procedure, and notable event, the ledger was spotless, detailed, and thorough.

Her grandfather's record-keeping was immaculate and well above reproach. By all evidence, his detail and wits both seemed in fine working order.

Contracts, payroll, purchases, and sales—her job would be an easy copycat procedure, mocking actions already a million times taken. Nothing mind-boggling, but good resume material all the same. Of course, the shared last name of Wade might paint an inaccurate picture. Her grandfather would cut her no breaks, but her future employers wouldn't know that.

It would be better if she could use Mac as her employer. By the looks of the books and all the large personal investments he'd already made, the passing of the reins was already in progress. Would he give her a fair recommendation? Yes, he probably would, but that would mean she'd have to be nice to him.

Her shoulders curled as the unpleasant thought held

its debut inside her head.

Gag. As she'd discovered last night, she wasn't *that* good of an actress.

She should probably work on her coping skills as she'd need the reference, and as things stood, this was her future, like it or not, for the next two years. At least the false act of politeness would provide her the challenge it appeared she was going to need. But before trying anything so drastic, she'd first make sure such a succession plan was actually in place. She wouldn't want to waste any "nice" on the man for nothing.

Hearing footsteps coming down the stairs, she glanced toward the door. What exactly was their plan for the changing of the guard? It seemed odd, when the matter was so important to both of them, that they wouldn't at least have discussed it.

She knew her grandfather would never want to leave. Would he set up the transfer upon his death or go forward with the transfer, setting in place a condition that would allow him to stay? Not that he'd ever really need such an agreement. No matter what else she thought of Mac, she knew his affections for her grandfather were real. Outside of no blood relation, the two were as much family as family could be.

Her grandfather had purchased Buster's Prairie from Mac's mother, Jenny Palmer, a woman who'd recently lost her husband to a tragic accident. His death, so completely unexpected, had shaken the young mother's world past the point of easy recovery. The ranch had faltered, debt became due. With no other options, and with one rather irregular agreement regarding its future sale, she'd sold the ranch to Grace's grandfather when Mac was not yet thirteen years old.

Both her grandparents had opened their hearts to the young widow and her two young sons, offering Jenny a job, home, and place to raise her boys. Over the years, they'd formed a bond that would never be broken.

Grace's father always said the boys were the sons his father had always wanted, and perhaps he was right. Gramps had never understood her father's fascination with archeology. *"Why waste your time digging around in someone else's past when you could be helping build your own future?"* he'd always say.

"Well?" her grandfather asked, suddenly appearing in the doorway and pulling her back to the present.

"Nice job, Grandpa." She tapped her nails against the ledger. "You've made my job very easy."

"Clean makes simple. Simple makes clean."

She smiled. "That's what Grandma always says."

"Your grandmother's a smart lady."

"Yeah." Grace pushed back her chair and stood. "She is." Stepping across the room, she took her grandfather's arm in hers. "You miss her, don't you?"

"Every day. How about a tour?" he said, changing the subject as he turned and led her toward the door.

"A tour? Grandpa, I've lived here most of my life."

"Four years is a long time. A lot has changed. Have you seen the new chutes?"

"From a distance." Grace grabbed her tan cowboy hat from the decorative wall-rack hanging beside the door. She had two, one tan and one black. Much to her surprise, she'd found them both exactly where she'd left them four years earlier. She adjusted the hat then smiled at her grandfather. "I wouldn't mind a closer look."

A few minutes later, they had circled the new pens and were standing near the gravel drive admiring all the changes.

"They look fantastic." And she meant it. She'd watched the roundups enough through the years to know the improvements made sense. "It's a great set up."

"The design is Mac's, and it's a good one, too. It's made things much easier and safer for both the handlers and the cattle."

Pushing her hands into the back pockets of her jeans, she merely nodded. *Yep, Wonder Boy is utterly brilliant.* The man literally could do no wrong. Oh yeah, except for the part where he helped her fiancé decide to dump her and marry another.

"Watch this." Her grandfather walked over to the chute's duel-sided gates. "Check out how easily these work." With obvious pride, he commenced giving her a demonstration. As one side opened, the other side gave a nice little squeeze that would move its occupant forward, the goal being a steady and smooth progression in and out of the passageway.

Grace leaned against its metal frame. "Nice."

"Pretty snazzy, all right." Her grandfather's grin faded somewhat as he spotted riders in the distance. "Looks like the boys are back."

The boys ended up being Mick, Phil, and Jarrod. They arrived a few minutes later toting the two stray horses Mac had spotted the day before out on the range.

Gramps tilted back his hat as they approached and eyed their two new companions. "Any markings?"

Mick road up closer to the first horse—a chestnut-colored quarter horse who took his approach far too calmly to be anything but domesticated. The young ranch hand pulled back the horse's mane to display a pair of white angel wings freezer-branded high on the horse's neck.

"Bill Ryan," her grandfather said with a touch of surprise.

The rancher owned Angels & Saints Ranch down near Hereford—not a small distance from Buster's Prairie.

"Yep." Phil patted the second horse—a golden-colored Palomino with a white mane. "Same for this fella. Nice horses. I imagine Bill's beside himself at the moment."

Gramps nodded. "I imagine he is. Wish I'd have thought to check the boards."

Like cows, horses occasionally got loose. Typically, they didn't wander too far, but every now and again they ended up somewhere surprising. Usually, you'd hear about them on the online boards monitored regularly by the local ranchers or if not there, through word of mouth.

Phil gave the Palomino another pat before leaning back in his saddle. "I'll give Bill a call. Let him know we've got 'em."

"I'd appreciate that." Gramps gave the group an appreciative wave. "Thanks, men. Good work."

After tilting their hats in farewell, the three cowboys, along with the ranch's two newest guests, continued on toward the corral.

Her grandfather watched them a silent moment before turning her way. "Well, there's a happy ending."

Grace grinned. "I don't know. I was kinda' hoping we could keep 'em."

His face lit with both affection and amusement. "You always were partial to strays."

"I've often felt like a stray myself. Luckily, you and Grandma were softies and always took me in." She looked around the yards. "So, what's next on the agenda?"

"Thought I'd take you to the barn and introduce you to another group of squatters."

"Squatters."

"A nice little family. I think you're going to like them." His lip quirked, assuring her there was a little more behind it than his words might suggest.

"All right."

As they made their way across the yard to the old, weathered barn, Grace searched the pens and corral for any sign of the sand-colored curls she couldn't, despite her best efforts, get out of her head.

Garrett's hair would curl, but only when it was wet, and it never had been the same loose, untamed, and painfully sexy look Mac's always carried. Always. He'd always had those curls that turned women's heads and fed their fantasies…or at least they'd fed hers until she'd fallen in love with his brother.

Realizing she was searching him out, she forced herself to look forward the rest of the way.

What was wrong with her anyway? Back but a day, and already he was messing things up for her, working his way into her thoughts with those hard-to-forget eyes and that lazy, self-confident smile. How could she let him affect her like this? The man had done nothing but turn her dreams into ashes. She should be able to despise him past attraction. Respect herself enough to never again allow him close enough to hurt her.

The barn doors were already wide open as they approached. The old clunker of a truck that had driven her home from the airstrip sat jacked up in the middle of the structure, a pair of feet hanging out its right side.

Bracing himself along the side of the truck, Gramps leaned down to yell underneath. "Find the problem?"

From behind the feet, two long legs emerged followed by a rock-hard body, grease-stained face, and unfortunately, the same sand-colored curls she'd been hunting in the yard.

"She's old, practically begging to retire, but new U-joints will hold her for now."

"Old, but not out," Gramps said with a grin. "Don't give up on her yet, son."

"My talents only go so far. If we wait much longer, we're going to be stuck with nothing more than an old log of metal to rot in our yards. We need to get rid of her and get another."

"I'll give it some thought." Her grandfather rubbed the truck's side in a manner resembling reassurance.

Mac looked Grace's way then nodded behind her. "The pups are over there. Tilly will growl, but she won't actually bite."

"Puppies?" She practically yelped as she twirled on her toes and headed toward the back. Everyone knew puppies were her weakness.

Tucked in the far-right corner of the barn, a small, make-shift kennel had been squared-off with haystacks. Inside, a very tired looking Kelpie lay on her side allowing five adorable babes to suckle.

"Look at your beautiful babies, Till." Taking a seat on one of the haystacks, she watched the little black and brown bundles of fur.

"Funny looking things, aren't they?" her grandfather said over her shoulder.

"They're precious. I want one."

"Already spoken for. Every one of 'em."

"*Ohhh.* Any for here?"

"Mac's got dibs on that chubby boy there." He pointed to the biggest bundle hanging tight to his claim in the middle of the pack.

"Why him specifically?"

"He was the one that was left."

Mac's timber-like drawl rolled down her back, causing a jolt of awareness that tingled its way straight to her core, thrilling yet unwelcomed.

Grace braced herself and glanced back over her shoulder. He was standing beside her grandfather with a white work cloth moving between his hands. A long, unattended dab of grease ran the course of his nose. She grinned but said nothing.

They watched the greedy pups feed a while longer before her grandfather sighed and patted her shoulder. "I've a job for the two of you."

Grace's senses went on full alert. *A job for the two of them* sounded a lot like *alone time*, and that was something she'd planned to avoid.

"William Baxter's selling a couple of four wheelers," her grandfather continued. "He's letting us have first look at them, but he's not willing to wait."

Mac nodded. "We could definitely use them."

"Agreed. That's why you and Grace are heading that way now to take a look. If they're decent, we want 'em. It'll save us a bundle upfront as well as the expense of hauling them back from the city."

It was a good hour to the Baxter's, probably more. That would be way too much time trapped with a man she'd have to work to be nice to.

Grace moistened her suddenly dry lips. "Do we both need to be there?"

Her grandfather's piercing gray eyes narrowed with annoyance as his gaze zoomed right in on her. "The office manager does. Is that you?"

"Well, yes, but…certainly this is a job easily handled by one."

"You think you can handle it all on your own?" A heavy brow lifted in mirth, suggesting he thought otherwise.

Shifting her weight, she shot a glance in Mac's direction. His arms were crossed, his focus on her. At that moment, he looked so incredibly hot, she thought about backtracking. Thankfully, she was armed with a full history of reasons to ignore his appeal.

Shaking her head, she turned her attention to her grandfather. "I…I didn't mean that I should—"

"Good news, Mac," Gramps interrupted her trip across her own tongue before slapping the younger man's shoulder. "Sounds like Grace has this one covered. Apparently, you're off the hook—free for the evening."

Mac merely cast him a wary look and sighed.

"Oh," her grandfather added, turning back to Grace, one finger raised, like an afterthought, high in the air, "you'll want to take the one-ton and hitch the trailer. There's no sense making two trips if they seem a good deal." Turning around, he headed across to the barn's entrance where he pulled the one-ton's keys from a post full of the notched and grooved devices.

"Make sure you load the ramps as well," he instructed, marching back her way. "And be certain to set their clamps so that they're tight." He dangled the keys in front of her nose. "Those bikes can be heavy. They'll knock those ramps right off the trailer if the clamps aren't set right. A pint-sized lassie like you sure wouldn't want one of those bikes rolling 'em under."

Grace took a deep breath then exhaled. Her grandfather always had preferred the long route in teaching a lesson. She ignored the keys. "All right, Grandpa. I get it."

He tilted his head. "What's that, dear?"

"I'm going, and I need help."

"You do?" He feigned surprise. "Hmm, you better check with Mac and make sure he can still make it. By now, he may have made other plans."

Mac rolled his eyes, grabbed the keys, and then looked to Grace. "Grab the checkbook and some water. I'll go get the truck."

Feeling every bit as ridiculous as her grandfather had hoped she would, she actually managed a smile. "Thank you."

"Yep," he said, turning around and heading out.

Okay, she had to admit it. He was being pretty gracious, all things considered. Turning back around to face her antagonist, she nearly startled at his fiery expression.

"All right, Grace Elizabeth, out with it. What is it you have against that man?"

The list was long, but the portion she was willing to share was relatively short. "You mean other than his destroying my relationship with Garrett?"

He dropped his head, shaking it regretfully. "If

Garrett had loved you enough, nothing would have stopped him from marrying you. I know you don't see it, but that man," he said, pointing in the direction Mac had headed, "did you a favor."

"A favor?" A vein twitched at the base of her neck, right above the lump of indignation lodged in her throat. It had always hurt her bitterly that both her grandparents insisted there was no blame to be laid. "How can you side with him, Grandpa?"

"He saw his brother about to make a mistake, and he spoke his mind. I can't fault him for that."

"A mistake," she repeated.

Her expression must have registered the hurt, for her grandfather's face instantly fell. "Wait a minute, Grace. That's not a judgment on you."

"I've got to go." Turning her cowboy boots toward the barn doors, she made for a quick escape.

"Grace, honey, you're taking it all wrong."

Her grandfather's words followed her out the open doors. Maybe he was right, but she had a feeling she understood it better than he realized. She'd been hearing the word long enough, she'd come to understand well its various connotations. First there were her parents who'd never planned on having kids. Sure, they loved her, but the fact remained they hadn't wanted her. It was a truth often emphasized by their long absences and her frequent stays with her grandparents. Then there was Garrett who had chosen her, promised her forever, then simply changed his mind.

She was tired of being *a mistake.* It would be really great if, for once, someone would look at her and say, *"Wow, Grace, you're the best thing that ever happened to me."*

Wouldn't that be special?

****

After taking each bike for a ride, Mac walked from one to the next, checking the CV boots, air filters, electrical components, shocks and looking for leaks—pretty much searching for anything that might pose a problem. But just as he'd suspected, the only crime the quads had committed was growing another year older.

William Baxter liked the newest and best, which equated to good-fortune for his neighbors and closest friends.

"We'll take them both." Mac stepped back around the bikes and past Grace to offer Baxter his hand. "Thanks, William. We appreciate the offer."

"And I appreciate dealing with those who know a good deal and are willing to pay for it upfront." The rancher took his hand and squeezed it tight. "Can't take the bargaining some want to do, nor do I care for holding debt."

"Debt between neighbors is no better an idea than debt between friends," Mac said with a grin.

"Amen to that, young man." Nodding his head over his shoulder toward the house, William asked the two of them to follow him. "Claire's been near giddy since she heard Grace was coming with you. She insisted I bring you both inside for tea and a little catch up. I'll give you fair warning though. You're going to get an ear-bashing about the social she and Tess are hosting here at the end of the month."

Gravel popped beneath their feet as they made their way across the drive to the Baxter's side door.

"Single and attractive, neither one of you is going

to be let off easy." William stopped once they reached the house. "To be honest, if I had to make a wager, my money would be on my wife. That woman has her ways, God bless her." He chuckled as he turned the knob and opened the door for them to lead the way.

Mac waited for Grace to enter then followed right behind her.

He'd been to the ranch several times through the years and knew the entire family well—well enough to know William was right. If Claire had set her sights on filling her dance floors, there was little hope he or Grace would leave the place uncommitted.

One short hallway and a turn later, they were standing behind a large breakfast bar looking into a spacious kitchen. Two bottoms—both in denim, one plump and one nicely rounded—greeted them from outside an open oven.

"What do you think, two maybe three more minutes?" the youngest Ms. Baxter asked as both ladies studied the enticement they had baking inside.

"Two," came the reply, "then we'll take another look."

"Ah hmm," William vied for the attention of his wife and daughter, a humored grin spreading wide across his face.

In a rather comical fashion, both heads turned their way, popping out from in front of the rears. Spotting them, both women gasped and stood to full height.

"Well, that had to be quite a sight." Claire brushed her only-now graying strawberry bangs back away from her forehead. After wiping her hands across her jeans, she headed their way. "Mac, always good to see you." She offered him her hand.

He ignored it and gave her a hug.

Still standing in front of the stove, her daughter, Tess, grinned. "Handsome," she greeted him while lifting her foot behind her and kicking closed the oven door.

"Good to see you, Tess."

Nineteen years old, the young woman was just short of a knockout—tall, strawberry blonde with an adorable smile to fit her spirited personality. If the tales he'd been hearing were true, she had it "bad" for his newest recruit, Lance Poe. The young cowboy wasn't yet so smitten, but Mac had a feeling time would soon change that. Give the young lady a year or two, and she'd no doubt blossom fully into the beauty all indicators registered waiting. Then Lance's head would turn, and hopefully not too late.

"Hope it's something sweet you two were eyeing inside that oven," he teased, knowing full well if Claire had been expecting company, she'd been baking something up. Mrs. Baxter was as notorious for her baked goods as she was for her hospitality.

"Chocolate chip cookies, and I've got the teapot already starting to boil. We have raspberry, caramel, and cinnamon teas to choose from. Tell me you'll stay and visit a spell."

"Careful," her husband warned, sending a wink their way.

Flicking a dismissive hand over her shoulder, Claire reached past Mac to squeeze Grace's arm. "So good to see you, dear."

"Lovely to see you again, Mrs. Baxter, and believe me, I could never say no to freshly baked chocolate chip cookies, especially yours. I remember them well."

Beaming with pride, Claire stepped around Mac to stand closer to Grace. "Sweetie, I wouldn't have thought it possible, but I believe you're even more beautiful than I remembered. I'll bet you've got those poor ranch hands at your place tripping over their own two feet to impress you. Am I right?"

"Not at all." With her cheeks toting an obvious blush, Grace dipped her chin low.

Claire winked his way. "She's being modest, isn't she, dear?"

The little vixen certainly had him tripping over his, but that was a truth he wouldn't be sharing.

Not waiting for an answer, Mrs. Baxter took Grace's hand and his and guided them to the breakfast table sitting in front of the kitchen's window. "Now, take a seat. Tess and I will pull a tray together and be right over."

"Remember my warning." William smiled their way but still managed to pat his wife's backside as she passed. "They're going to sweeten you up then force feed you their agenda."

"William Baxter," Claire scolded, "if you can't make yourself useful in here then go make yourself useful elsewhere."

He merely pulled out a chair to swing it around and straddle. "I might actually find myself useful, love. For the sake of our guests, I believe I'll stay."

Thirty minutes later, despite William's best attempts to run interference, Mac found himself, as well as his men, committed to attending the upcoming social. Grace hadn't fared any better, though it was hardly surprising. Seeming somewhat distracted through the entire conversation, she'd practically helped set herself up. He was certain it wasn't intentional, however, as she'd seemed more than a little surprised to find herself lassoed.

Now, watching her stare blankly out the truck's windshield at the long road ahead, he wondered exactly what was bothering her. "Is everything all right?"

Her lids batted up and down as though she'd forgotten she wasn't alone. She turned her lovely blue gaze his way. "Tess has certainly grown into a beautiful woman."

Expecting a snide and dismissive remark, he was surprised by the comment, as well as the calm demeanor in which it was delivered. He nodded. "Yes, she has."

Pursing her lips, Grace tapped her fingers against the titles she now held in her hands. "*Woman* is probably not the right word," she pondered out loud. "How old is she now—eighteen? Nineteen?"

"Nineteen," he replied, turning his attention back to the road.

Grace sighed and bounced the sheets against her knees before placing them up on the dashboard. "Really more a child than a woman…wouldn't you say?"

He shot another glance her way, curious as to exactly what she was getting at. "I'd say that depends on the woman. What's your point, Grace?"

"Point?" She scowled, her calm demeanor turning instantly to the defensive. "I'm just saying she's young."

He had a feeling there was a little more behind it than that, but couldn't imagine it being interesting enough to warrant the further ruffling of her feathers.

They drove a few more minutes in silence before

she shifted in her seat to face him. "It seemed very important to her that you be at the dance."

"Huh? Oh, yeah, I guess it did."

"So, you noticed?"

It appeared silence was going to work as well as digging. Whatever it was brewing behind that lovely head of hers was festering to get out. "Guests are scarce in this area. Since I bring with me a small herd, I'm a pretty popular guy." He tossed her a sheepish grin. Typically, with most women, it would at least win him a smile. Not true with Miss Wade. Instead, her lips remained still, her look...bothered.

"She likes you."

And the troublesome thorn has finally broken through.

Tess' only interest lay in Lance, but Grace's interest interested Mac. It actually interested him a great deal.

"Do you think so?" He pulled his brows and puckered his lips as though giving it serious thought. "Maybe," he finally replied, turning back to the road. "Are you jealous?"

"Jealous?" she sputtered, her hands flying up to cover her heart as though it might explode from the shock. "Of course not. *Jealous.* What a ridiculous idea. I'm simply saying you should be careful. She's young, too young to know what it is she really wants."

"I won't argue that, but I should probably point out that she's the exact age you were when you first became engaged to Garrett."

Heavily lashed lids blinked across startled blue eyes. Once again, those tantalizing lips pursed as she gave his words consideration. "I imagine that's true, though I think that's a little different. I'd known Garrett near my whole life."

"I've known Tess her entire life. What does that have to do with anything?"

Her eyes widened, and her lips opened as though she were about to speak. She held the pose a moment before biting down on her lower lip and staring back out the window.

He couldn't help himself; he smiled.

Grace caught sight of the grin and visibly bristled. "What?"

"What do you mean *what*? Do you mean, why the smile?"

Her brow furrowed as her head slightly tilted to a defensive angle. "Yes."

He shrugged his shoulders. "I find it humorous, I guess."

"You find *what* humorous exactly?"

Shaking his head, he chuckled. "I find it humorous that you see the point but refuse to acknowledge it. You've always been like that, you know. So headstrong-stubborn you leap right over the obvious to get back to the same dead-end trail."

"Just because I don't see an issue, it doesn't necessarily mean I'm avoiding it. I simply tend to, as a rule, step around stupid. So, what's your point?"

"My point is you and Garrett were both too young back then to know your minds. *You* weren't ready to make such an important decision, any more than he."

"Garrett was twenty-one, and I have always known my mind far better than most."

The problem was, she really believed it.

He shot her a doubtful glance. "Being a dreamer is

entirely different from knowing your mind. *You*, Grace Wade, were not only too young to make such an adult decision—you were also far too naïve."

Cold, blatant hatred flashed from her eyes. "Naïve? Just because *you* didn't agree with our decision, that doesn't make it naïve."

"No, but the fact it was made by two impetuous kids who were more in love with the idea of getting married than they were with each other, certainly does."

A shocked and furious gasp filled the cab. "Stop the truck."

"I'm not stopping the truck."

"I'm leaving this truck whether it's moving or not." Her hand hovered threateningly over the handle.

Knowing her well enough to know her temper often aced her common sense, he stopped the truck. "You're not close enough to anything to walk anywhere," he said as he watched her pull back the handle. "What exactly do you think you're going to do—catch a ride on an armadillo?"

She didn't hesitate for a moment and pushed against the door.

He made one last attempt. "Go ahead if you like, but I better warn you. Cooked by the sun, you're going to smell mighty tasty to some of the wildlife around these parts."

"I'll take my chances." Swinging her legs toward out, she shot him one last contemptuous snarl over her shoulder before making her exit.

Dang, but if the woman couldn't teach a mule a thing or two about stubborn.

Banging his hands against the wheel, he gritted his teeth and cursed her unreasonableness. *A smart man would leave the minx to walk.* He took a deep breath. *A smart man would have known better than to poke a sensitive thorn.* His shoulders lifted and fell with a heavy sigh. *A smart man wouldn't allow himself to care.*

Pushing open his door, he jumped out onto the dirt-hardened path.

A heart-felt curse rang from behind the trailer.

That was his Grace, not exactly a delicate flower.

His Grace—funny how the thought came so easily to mind.

Placing his hat back on his head, he moved toward the sounds of grumbling.

"A dreamer," she mocked, bent over the trailer's tailgate. "I have a dream all right, and it doesn't include this place or his know-it-all opinion." She was talking to herself as she fought with the latch keeping the gate secure. "It must be nice to know everyone and everything so perfectly well, to always have the answer to what is and isn't right. Why, it should be a job." For the first time, she looked his way. "Oh, wait. It is, isn't it? It's God's." Her upper lip twitched with disdain. "News flash, Palmer—that's *not* you."

She bent back over the rail.

Mac ignored the taunt and looked instead to the four wheelers. Great, apparently Funny Lady figured out an escape route. "All right, sweetheart, do you even know how to ride one of these things?"

Pushing back the hair that had fallen forward across her face, she looked up only long enough to award him an unfriendly glare before returning her attention to the uncooperative metal.

Crossing his arms over his chest, he leaned his

weight back onto his heels and watched her struggle. "They're not the same as the dirt bikes we used to ride. They're tricky. They take the terrain entirely different."

Taking a new hold on the latch, she fumbled with it once more before grunting with frustration and simply shaking the railing in a temper.

"That'll do it," he mocked.

Fierce blue eyes pierced him with contempt. "If you're not going to help, kindly remain silent." Looking back down to the latch, she finally took the time to study its hold. Pulling the railing toward her, she released enough pressure from the handle to pop its lock.

He should have known she'd find a way. With a will like few others, she probably would heist a bike and tear it across the hills just to prove her point. She'd probably even make it home.

But that wasn't a chance he was willing to take.

Stepping past her onto the trailer, he made for the bikes then pulled the keys out of each.

"Are you kidding me?" She still stood at the tail of the trailer, fists on hips, teeth clenched in fury.

"Better get in the truck, Grace, before you burn that hotheaded noggin of yours to a crisp."

She grabbed for the keys as he stepped back down onto the dirt road.

Lifting them high into the air, he easily dodged her attempts. "Good plan. Got another?"

"Those are my grandfather's bikes. I can ride them if I want to." Making an impressive jump, she came surprisingly close to reaching the dangling brass.

"I'm pretty sure your grandfather would disagree." He moved the keys to the hand farthest away from his abnormally limber opponent. "Now, that's enough, Grace. I said, get in the truck."

A spark of something that looked a whole lot like trouble danced in her eyes.

A knot of unease formed in his stomach. "Grace, I wouldn't—"

Then, exactly that fast, she made a U-turn and headed for the cab.

He was right on her heels. He knew her a little too well. If he wouldn't give her the quads, she'd take the whole truck. And he knew from past experience, she'd have no problem leaving him stranded.

She'd nearly reached the driver's door before he caught her, pulled her around, and trapped her against the truck. "Not gonna happen, sweetheart."

Hair tousled and eyes a tad wild—she shoved her open palms against his chest. "You're such an ass!"

Mac grabbed her wrists and pulled her hands behind her, bringing her body snug against his. "You really need to come up with better material. You're slipping, Grace." Even through his frustration, it was impossible to miss how wonderful she felt against him. Hellcat or not, the woman fit him like a comfy pair of jeans.

She struggled to get free, but he held on tight.

Finally, she surrendered and simply slapped her palms against his chest. "If the material didn't fit you so well, maybe I would."

He pulled her even closer. "You're only mad because you know I'm right."

She gasped at their proximity, but quickly recovered to fight back. "You're wrong. Garrett loved me. He loved me until you started questioning his reasoning, questioning his feelings for me. And let's not forget the act that took the win—introducing him to Jackie. Brilliant. I have to hand it to you, Palmer. You're nothing if not determined."

Guilt stepped forward, lodging itself as a painful knot at the back of his throat. Up until that moment, he hadn't realized she knew.

He took a deep breath and considered his next words carefully. "I wish I could tell you I regret it, but I don't. Jackie's been good for him."

"And you're so sure I wouldn't have been?"

The hurt in her eyes was nearly more than he could stand, but he'd come too far to back down. "Believe it or not, I only questioned his feelings because he'd shown doubt. And marrying you because *you* wanted it was never a good reason. Fact is, Grace, you spent so many years plotting your happily-ever-after, you forgot to ask the cast if they still wanted their roles."

Her chin quivered. She swallowed hard, but when she spoke, her voice was still rough with anguish. "Garrett wasn't forced. *He* asked me, remember? It was *your* mind that wasn't settled, *your* thoughts that got him confused." She looked down, no doubt trying to hide the tears he'd already seen brimming at the corners of her eyes.

"I didn't drive him into her arms. I know that makes it easier to believe, but it isn't true." Letting go of her wrists, Mac moved to wipe a tear from her cheek.

She immediately swatted his hand away.

He sighed and took a step back. "When are you going to see it?" Raking a hand through his hair, he stared at her a silent, hopeless moment. "When are you finally going to open your eyes and admit it was never meant to be?"

She flinched, moistening her lips. "Says you."

"No, Grace, says Garrett. He's my brother. Don't you think we've talked about this a time or two? Believe it or not, the doubts in my mind came first from his."

A sharp sob purged from her throat as her chest heaved with its power. She turned around, wiping fiercely at the tears now rolling as a tell-all down her face. "He loved me. I know he did."

"Yes, but not enough, not in the way a man should love the woman he binds himself to for the rest of his days. It wouldn't have been fair to either one of you. Think about it, Grace. Would you want to be married to a man who couldn't give you his full heart?"

She shook her head—first in denial, and then, slowly, something changed. He could see it in her stance, in the way her shoulders fell. Her breath caught, the shakes of her head slowed.

"No," she said in the form of a whisper. The sadness in her voice pierced like an arrow. Then she raised her chin, took a deep breath. "No," she repeated with a great deal more conviction.

His heart pounded with hope. He took a step closer but stopped when she stiffened. "You deserve better, Grace. You deserve someone who'll love you beyond the point of any doubts. Someone who'll wake up every morning knowing he's the luckiest man alive. Believe me, there are plenty of men who would love the role. Garrett simply wasn't one of them."

She didn't reply, but he sensed, for the first time in years, she was actually listening.

"The ranch meant a lot to you. I understand why

Garrett seemed so right. But…" He paused, placing his hands on her turned shoulders. "Love isn't about finding someone who'll fit your dreams. Love is about finding someone who'll help you build them." It was a piece of advice his mother had once given him, good advice as it turned out.

She took a shaky breath. "The ranch was the only stability I'd ever known. I was happy there." Anguish played across her face as she turned back around. "I loved Garrett. I did. But…" She closed her eyes. "Maybe some of it was my simply wanting to belong."

He'd never wanted to take anyone in his arms more in his life, but this was new ground. He wasn't about to do anything that might make it crumble. "You do belong. You always have, but that has nothing to do with Garrett."

Lids lifted and bright blue eyes looked up to stare into his—sad, lost. "It's not my home."

"It *is* your home, yours and your grandparents'."

A heartbreaking smile played across her lips like a weak signal upon a screen. "No matter what the papers say, any fool can see the ranch belongs to you, always has, always will."

Her words held some truth. He simply couldn't bring himself to deny it. "It's still your home just as it's Eldon's."

"It was my home, and when I needed a home so badly. Maybe that's why I loved it so much, why I held on so tightly."

"What do you mean *loved*? Grace, you still love the ranch." He was surprised at how much the past tense threw him, but it did. Grace's love for the ranch was one of the most endearing traits about her, always had been, though he may not have always appreciated it as such.

"I love the people. I love what the ranch has meant to me, but I no longer believe it's the only place worthy on Earth. I'm ready to branch out, ready to try new places. I guess it's fair to say I'm ready to move on." She smiled. "Good news for you, right? You get your land and no obnoxious tag-along."

His heart lurched. "Good news? No!" A surprising sense of panic swelled from his chest to nearly choke him. "I mean, you're welcome to stay at the ranch as long as you like...and expected to," he quickly added, "for the next two years anyway."

"Two years," she repeated while running her hands through her hair. The look on her face wasn't so much sadness this time as resignation. She sighed and shrugged her shoulders. "Speaking of moving on, we should probably get back."

"Huh? Oh, yeah." He stepped back and let her step away, around the truck and back into the cab.

After struggling to get her to listen for so long, he should feel better than he did. But he didn't. His determination seemed to have rolled straight past success into a surprising sense of desperation.

He had two years—two years to figure out why the "crazy" she made him was starting to feel so good.

Chapter Seven

Grace picked a handful of grass and waved it over the fence. "Come on, girl."

Dolly, a dark-chocolate spotted American Paint Horse, and her favorite horse in years gone by, stood still in the middle of the pasture working a mouthful of the very same grass around her lower jaw. She watched Grace, but seemed mostly indifferent.

"Oh, come on, Dolly, don't be like that."

Romeo and Starlet, standing closer to the fence, lifted their long buckskin necks from the pasture's floor then turned their backs to her and walked farther out into the pasture.

Slumping against the fence, she sighed. "Seriously, guys? You haven't seen me in four years. What's with the cold shoulders?"

"They haven't seen you in four years," a deep and all-too-familiar drawl rang from behind her.

Grace shaded her eyes and turned back toward the morning sun. There, framed by a perfectly blue Texas sky, stood Mac.

"Here, try this," he said, holding out a green plastic bucket.

With a peculiar mix of excitement and frustration, she gave her best girl-powered try at not ogling his prime-grade bod'. Unfortunately, he wasn't cooperating. Dressed in a nice-fitting pair of Wranglers, which hugged his impressive thighs as though they'd been built just for him, and a casually worn denim shirt, which covered but didn't completely hide his touch-me-please chest, he looked hot, cowboy-hot.

Her pulse stepped up its pace.

"They can be fickle." He nodded toward her grazing friends. "And they like the morning's dew-kissed grass. You'll probably have to coax them." He wiggled the bucket. "Grain mixed with molasses. It's their favorite."

In other words—bait, something she should have thought to do.

"I'm not above bribing." Grace smiled and took the bucket. "Thanks." When she turned back around, all three horses were staring. "Right, I see how you are. Come on then. Come and get it." Reaching into the bucket, she pulled out a handful of grain and held it out over the fence.

Romeo never hesitated, and seeing him move, Starlet quickly followed. But Dolly merely lifted her nose and snorted.

Grace looked back over her shoulder to Mac. "What's up with her?"

He shrugged his shoulders. "Not real sure. Maybe she's mad at you for staying gone so long."

"No." She shook her head and looked back to her friend. Dolly was watching her, but still not moving. "Do you really think that's it?"

Mac moved up to the fence to stand beside her. "I don't know, but horses have big hearts. You could have bruised hers a little." Reaching inside the green pail, he pulled out a handful of grain and offered it to Romeo.

Romeo was Mac's horse, and it was apparent by

the gelding's gentle nuzzle over the post that he loved his master.

Starlet came to Grace, brushing her snout against her palm as she fed.

"Hey, Miss Starlet." She petted the mare's long muzzle with her free hand. "I see you still have Romeo following at your heels."

"Were you not paying attention?" Mac asked. "It's the other way around." Leaning over the fence, he gave Romeo a pat. "Huh, boy? The ladies can't get enough of you."

Grace laughed as the horse lifted his head out of Mac's hand and actually nodded.

"No way! How did you get him to do that?"

He merely smiled and offered his buddy more grain.

"I'd be careful of that one, Starlet," she warned as the mare finished cleaning out her palm. "Such ego could leave a girl little air to breathe."

Mac turned back her way, giving her a shameless grin. "It's not ego. It's fact. The ladies love Romeo…or maybe it's his handsome rider," he teased.

She rolled her eyes and pulled back her *cleaned* palm to wipe it against her jeans. "Maybe you're the one who better be careful, braggart. That big head of yours might topple you right over into the pasture."

Stepping away from the fence, Mac moved to stand directly in front of her. "Worried about me, Grace?"

He was close. Close enough she could smell the intoxicating mix of a musk-scented aftershave, clean earth-scented soap, and a baseline scent of totally male. If he'd have turned at that moment and walked off, it was quite possible she'd have pulled a Starlet and followed.

Luckily, he only smiled and grabbed back the green bucket. "Come on, sweetheart. Let's go butter up a mare."

"I really wish you'd quit calling me that," she mumbled, but this time, it was only half-heartedly. Truth be told, the endearment was starting to hit her a little too comfortably.

She followed him between the fence posts and out into the pasture, excitement keeping her practically skipping behind him. Somewhere along the short journey, she realized it wasn't all about the horse.

Watch it, Grace.

Maybe things could be better between them, but she wouldn't allow herself to go there. Like pouring whiskey on an empty stomach, giving her heart to this cowboy was simply a bad idea. But that didn't mean she couldn't check out those Wranglers as they plowed across the field.

Mmm hmm, nice.

Nope, it didn't mean that at all.

The Wranglers slowed. Grace redirected her sights.

Dolly, who'd long since gone back to grazing, lifted her head and warily watched them approach.

Mac took out a handful of grains and held them out in front of him. "You want your share, don't you, Dolly?"

The mare's head bobbed slightly. She took a tentative step forward.

"That's it, girl. Come say hello to Grace."

Dolly ignored her and headed for the bucket.

Grace's heart ached a little. It wasn't easy being shunned by a friend she'd held so dear.

Mac held out the pail Grace's way. She took a handful of grain and stepped hesitantly forward, fearful the mare might change her mind and retreat.

"All right." Mac stepped back to stand behind her. "Now, it's up to you."

She took a deep breath and stepped forward, holding out her filled palm in offering. "Want a treat, girl?"

Dolly stretched her neck to sniff then quickly took a step forward and dropped her head into Grace's palm.

"That a girl," she said, stepping forward to gently pet the horse's side. "You remember me, don't you, Dolly?"

The mare took a mouthful of grain then turned her head back to Grace's shoulder. She sniffed then blew out a snort of warm air. At first, she thought her friend would blow her off, but instead, Dolly nudged her nose against Grace's ear, pushing a few strands inside, tickling her with her own tresses.

Forgiveness or remembrance—Grace wasn't really sure which she was witnessing, but she knew it felt wonderful. She gave Dolly a huge hug, whispering promises of time they'd spend together.

Another palm full of grains gone, she and Mac headed back to the gate.

"Thank you," she said, squeezing between the fence posts.

"Glad to be of help." He passed the bucket her way before scaling the fence to join her. "Did you get a chance to ride much while in Vancouver?"

"Not at all. I didn't know anyone there with horses, and in truth, there simply wasn't the time. School kept me pretty busy."

"Out here you'll have plenty of opportunity and one huge arena to ride in. That's one thing about the ranch—even work can feel like play. There's none of that life-in-the-fast-lane madness that picks you up and takes over your life only to spit you out at retirement—exhausted, changed, and with too few memories you want to look back on."

Like her grandfather, Mac loved his piece of paradise.

She nodded. "The ranch is a goldmine for the cowboy-at-heart. I won't argue that. But your view of life in the city is perhaps a bit skewed. Not everyone lives in the fast lane. Plenty find their oasis right in the suburbs and sometimes in the heart of the city."

"Is that so?"

"Take my parents for example. They love the city—the many cultural attractions, the fine eating, the entertainment. They love knowing that when they leave for one of their finds, all they have to do is lock their apartment and everything will be fine until they return."

"My point exactly." He pointed happily at the invisible fact. "They have to leave their home and fly thousands of miles away to pursue their passion. Here, it's right outside our door."

"If ranching is your passion."

"Or good-quality, clean living in one of the most beautiful places on earth. You loved it here, Grace—the land, the lifestyle. I'm having a hard time believing that's changed simply by your gaining a couple letters to hang at the end of your name."

She shook her head and started walking back toward the house. "It's more than just a couple letters. It's a bachelor's degree—a bachelor's degree that's only useful when there are jobs to be found."

"There's a job right here," he said, catching up to her.

Grace shot him an amused glance. "Despite what Grandfather says, there really isn't. You two have this covered."

"That doesn't mean we don't appreciate a hand."

All right, eye-candy, enough already.

She stopped in her tracks to look at him. "Mac, what is this? Are you still afraid I'm going to bolt? You have my passport, remember? You can rest easy. I'm not planning to hijack your plane and fly it back to Canada. For the next couple years anyway, this is home sweet home."

He took a deep breath, ran his hand through his hair, and then let the breath out slowly. "I just—" His eyes squinted as he stared down the dirt road behind her.

She was about to turn and take a look herself when his steel-blue gaze focused back on her.

"I want you to remember this place for what it really is and for what it's been to you," he said. "Not as a distorted memory made ugly by events you'd like to forget. You loved it here. You were happy."

She didn't entirely understand his concern, but by the look on his face, she knew it was genuine and knew her response was important to him. "I remember it all— the good and the bad. Though, I'll admit, those last few months clouded things for me for a while. But if it's any conciliation, I'm doing much better."

She'd had four long years to paint back over the early years with the gloom and resentment she felt at the end. But Mac was right. It was time to refurbish the past and see it for what it was.

Grace smiled. "I remember I loved riding."

An answering smile lit his already handsome face. "That's one thing we have in common." He looked behind her once more toward the dirt road leading to the ranch.

That's when she heard it—the purr of an engine. She turned around.

A burgundy one-ton hauling a shiny white horse trailer was nearing the ranch.

"Bill Ryan," Mac said, answering the question sitting posed at the tip of her tongue.

Right then, she spotted the white wings splayed across the truck's hood. It was the owner of Angels & Saints Ranch coming to collect his two runaways.

The vehicle pulled past the gates and headed their way, coming to a stop directly in front of them. The tinted window on the passenger side rolled down. A good-looking man, too young to be Bill Ryan, smiled their way. "Good morning."

"Morning," Mac responded, taking a step closer to the window. "Mac Palmer." He reached through the window and offered the man his hand before nodding back her way. "This is Grace Wade, the owner's granddaughter."

The man took off his hat and nodded to Grace. "Todd Ryan, Bill's son. Pleased to meet you." He looked back to Mac. "We actually met a couple years back at Leo Brown's place."

He gave the guy more consideration then nodded. "I remember. You're friends with Willy, Jackie's cousin."

Grace shifted uncomfortably. Leo Brown was

Jackie Brown's father, Garrett's father-in-law. If the cowboy had spent much time around their place, it was hard to say what tales he may have heard about her.

"I'll go check on the horses," she said, banking on the whole out-of-sight-out-of mind thing. Turning with the green bucket still in hand, she made a break for the stable where the two runaways were being kept.

She always had wondered what thought Garrett's wife had given her, or if she'd ever given her any thought at all. How much had she known about Grace? Had she talked about her? Had *they* talked about her? She'd wondered it often but never gave much thought to what they'd said to others, at least, not until now.

Rounding the long, steel building that made up the stable, Grace took hold of the opening's pull and slid back the heavy metal door. Light filtered into the structure from behind her.

The only two horses currently inside, their guests stood with their noses outside the first two stalls.

"You boys ready to go home?"

She stopped beside the first stall and offered the Palomino a palm full of grain. When the treat was gone, she gave him an affectionate pat then headed for the next stall. The occupant lifted his head and neighed, suggesting he should have been first. But when she offered him her penance, he quickly got off his *high horse* and accepted the grains.

Grace leaned in against him, giving him a hug. "I wasn't gonna forget you."

"Now, don't go spoiling those two delinquents," a deep voice instructed from the entrance. "They're already handfuls as it is."

She grinned and turned toward the new arrival.

Todd really was a handsome man—brown hair, brown eyes, nearly Mac's height, which she noticed as said cowboy walked up behind him.

"Maybe I'm merely bribing them to come back," she suggested.

The man's eyes sparked with amusement. "I can see where you'd be an enticement."

"I'll help you get them loaded." Scowl sitting heavy at the bridge of his nose, Mac stepped around the young Mr. Ryan and headed for the horses. "Wanna' give me a hand here, Grace?"

"Sure thing." She turned back to the stall where she stood.

One compartment over, Mac's movements were sharp and hurried. He seemed a bit testy—a big difference from his earlier demeanor. The change was disappointing. She'd been enjoying their time together. But at least this time, she knew his bad temper had nothing to do with her. Luckily, she'd made herself scarce.

As she took hold of the board securing the stall's gate, an arm reached around her.

"I've got this," Todd said, giving her a wink.

Really nice eyes.

She stepped back as Mac pulled the first horse out into the walkway. He nodded toward the entrance. "Why don't you follow me out and open up the trailer."

"Sure." Maybe she was wrong, but she was starting to think he was purposefully trying to keep her away from Todd. She couldn't imagine why, unless...

The hairs on the back of her neck began to bristle. Of course, that had to be it. He was afraid she was going to say something stupid about Jackie. Grace

121

found her own disposition starting to sour as she followed him out of the stable to the back of the trailer.

"You don't have to worry, you know," she assured him once they reached the truck. "I'm not going to say anything to him. It's over—done. I'm moving on, remember?"

Mac's brows pulled together, but this time, it looked less like a scowl and more like confusion. "What are you talking about?"

"I'm talking about this 'hurry and get Grace out of the way' thing you have going on. You're afraid I'm going to say something rude about Jackie, but I'm not. Believe it or not, I have a lot more class than that."

His head tilted slightly. He blinked. "I needed your help."

"Yeah, all right, if that's the claim you're staking," she regurgitated a phrase he'd once used against her. Then, grumbling her discontent, she opened the trailer's door.

Mac shook his head and led the horse inside.

The clanking of hooves announced Todd's arrival. Swallowing her anger, Grace turned and offered him a smile. "Did you give him a *what-for*?"

"Wouldn't do any good." He patted the horse's side. "This boy's too ornery to care about my opinion." He leaned over the four-legged rebel and offered her his hand. "We really appreciate you taking such good care of our boys. Is there anything we can do to repay you?"

"They were no trouble." Grace took his hand and shook it. "Let's call it a pass-it-on courtesy."

"I like that idea. If ever there's a calling, you can be assured we'll do exactly that." He didn't immediately let go of her hand. "So, Grace, do you live here, or are you just here on a visit?"

"Living here at the moment."

"A long moment or short?"

"That depends on your idea of short. I'm here for the next couple of years anyway."

"Well, that is good news," he said, finally letting go of her hand.

"It's all yours." Mac jumped out of the back of the trailer and motioned for the cowboy to move inside.

Todd nodded his head, but instead of moving, he focused back on Grace. "Two years is a long stretch of time. Any plans on how you'll stay busy?"

It had been a while since she'd been flirted with, at least by someone so confident, but she was pretty sure that's what was going on. "I haven't given it much thought, I guess."

"Let me give you a hand." Mac stepped forward and grabbed hold of the horse's halter, encouraging the gelding forward.

Todd merely let go of the lead rope to let him take over, and then turned his attention back to Grace. "Any chance you're into horse racing?"

"You may find this surprising, but I've never actually been."

"Really?" Wrapping his fingers around his chin, he shot her an incredulous stare. "You know," he drawled, "I'm pretty sure that's a crime."

Oh yeah, he was definitely flirting.

She laughed. "In Texas, maybe."

He leaned back on his heels and grinned. "Seriously, I think you've been robbed, but I think I might be able to help you. We have a couple horses set to race down in Grand Prairie in September. There's a group of us going down and—"

"They're ready to go." Mac burst out of the trailer to step directly between them. Facing Todd with his hands on his hips, he basically blocked her out. "I imagine you're anxious to be on your way," he encouraged.

The rancher's brown eyes widened in surprise. "Ah…"

Mac offered him his hand in a blatant *get lost.*

The baffled young Ryan glanced between him and Grace, eventually smiling and taking the extended hand. "It was nice seeing you again, Mac. Please tell Jackie and Garrett I said hello. And thank Eldon for me, will you?"

"Like Grace said, it really wasn't a problem."

For the life of her, she couldn't figure out why he was acting so weird—not to mention rude. Mac Palmer was never rude to anyone, unless it was her.

Todd chuckled lightly and moved around the trailer to crawl into his truck.

Grace followed with Mac at her heels. She thought about telling Todd she'd love to experience the horse races, but she had a feeling her saying anything could set back the peaceful alliance she and Mac had made.

"Nice meeting you, Grace," he hollered out his window. "If you're ever near Hereford, stop by."

"We'll do that," Mac interjected, tossing an arm around Grace's shoulders.

She shot him a disbelieving glance as the truck roared to life.

Todd tipped his hat. Still chuckling to himself, he started down the road.

Grace stepped out of Mac's hold to spin around

and glare at him. "*What* was *that*?"

He shrugged. "What was what?"

"*That*—the 'we'll do that' and the whole arm-around-the-shoulders thing."

"I'm looking out for you. You don't know him."

"And what—he's a bad guy? He seemed pretty harmless to me."

Mac took a deep breath, rubbed the back of his neck. "He's all right, I guess."

She blinked, more confused than ever. "So, why the big-brother act?"

The hand at his neck dropped to his side. "He was interested in you, Grace. Couldn't you tell?" He caught sight of Brody and Tagger heading for the storage shed. "They're going to need my help. I better give them a hand."

And just like that, he was gone.

Grace stood with her mouth slightly agape. A perfectly *all right* guy showed her some interest. Was she supposed to have a clue why that was a bad thing? For the life of her, she couldn't figure Mac's reasoning. Why would Todd Ryan's interest in her be of any interest to him?

Unless he's interested himself.

"Yeah...right." She laughed out loud.

Mac heard the incredulous laughter ringing behind him and hurried his steps to the storage sheds. He didn't need to witness her amusement, and he certainly couldn't afford any further probing. Lord only knew what stupid thing would fall from his mouth next.

"What was that?" she'd asked. *That,* he was well aware, was a sad case of juvenile behavior. He'd seen the spark in Todd's eyes and felt his first case of

jealousy in years. Todd Ryan would be many women's idea of a *real catch*. Whether or not he'd be Grace's wasn't something Mac wanted to test. He'd wanted Todd gone, and gone with the message that Grace was not available. Mac's actions were instinctual, possessive, and entirely out of line.

Grace wasn't his to claim. Regardless of how right it might feel. *That* wasn't a right she'd given him; which meant, in short, he'd just committed the exact crime she'd been accusing him of for years. He'd played lord over her love life and chased a man away. He was lucky all he'd gotten was her indignation. She could have easily brushed off his arm and made him look a fool. Thankfully, she hadn't, and for that, he was grateful. It would have served him right if he'd have gotten his nose slapped after sticking it in where it didn't belong.

"Hey, boss," Brody greeted him as he rounded the shed's corner.

The burly redhead with perpetually pink cheeks stood at the top of a haystack that sat under the shed's back awning.

Mac leaned back on his heels and looked up. "Want some help?"

"We'll always take help," said Tagger, who leaned against the handle of a pitchfork at the base of the stack, waiting for the first bale of hay to be tossed down.

"Was that Todd Ryan picking up the horses?" Brody asked.

"It was. Do you know him?"

"Somewhat. I roomed with him at the FFA conference in Dallas my senior year. Seemed like a nice enough guy, maybe a tad arrogant, but that was high school." Brody grinned. "Most of us were pretty sure of ourselves back then."

"He was hitting on Grace."

Brody's grin disappeared as he exchanged a quick glance with the other ranch hand.

Tagger, a six-foot-four replica of a young Johnny Cash, pushed back his hat and picked up Brody's grin. "Rubbed ya the wrong way, did it, boss?"

Brody snorted then roared with laughter as he leaned down, grabbed a bale of hay and tossed it down by Tagger's feet.

Mac scowled at one then the other. "What's so funny?"

"Not a thing." The tall hand's grin turned into a full-blown smile. "Did you tell him to back off?"

Basically he had, but he wasn't going to admit it. Obviously, they already thought him interested in Grace. He wondered what it was he'd done that had given them the right impression. He hated to think he was that easily read.

The sound of steps shifting stone sounded behind him.

Brody looked past Mac. "Morning, beautiful."

"Morning, handsome." Grace stopped beside Mac and smiled up to the ranch hand. "You quit fooling around up there, Brody St. Clair. I don't want to be picking no body parts out of the morning feed."

"Your concern moves me," he replied before bending down and grabbing another bale to toss over the side.

Tagger forked the first bale then packed it over to the well-weathered pickup sitting to the side of the shed. With a swing of his fork, he tossed the hay over the truck's side and into its bed.

Mac turned toward the shed. "I'll grab the mix." Unlike the grass the cattle grazed on in the hills, the hay alone wasn't enough to fill the beasts' bellies and provide them with the nutrients they needed. It had to be mixed with corn silage and minerals, items they kept inside, away from the elements.

When all their cattle were in from the hills, feed time was a much bigger production with tractors, lifts, and every man on deck. But at the moment, most of their cattle were still grazing. Only the dairy cows, and a few cattle in pens due to injuries or illness, needed to be fed. Feed time was a much simpler affair this time of year, and one Mac truly enjoyed. This was life on the ranch at its finest—easy, relaxed but still real-life survival. The work fed him like the hay fed the cattle. He needed it, just like Eldon, just like his men.

A shadow fell inside the shed as Mac scooped the silage and loaded it into the first of two wheelbarrows. Looking over his shoulder, he was surprised to see Grace leaning against the door's frame.

She nodded to the wheeled cart. "Want some help?"

She wants to help? After the morning's fiasco, he was a bit surprised she was even speaking to him. This was definitely a different Grace from the last couple of days. Maybe he hadn't messed things up too bad after all.

Relief lightened his mood. "Sure. Wanna grab the minerals while I scoop the silage?"

"Easy enough." She headed for the bins lining the structure's back walls.

In no time, the two wheelbarrows were full, and

they were on their way to the truck where four more bales had been added and all strings removed. Mac shoveled the mixture into the vehicle as the two ranch hands mixed it all together.

Grace stood to the side, watching them work as she grilled Brody and Tagger on their love lives.

He learned a bit himself. It turned out Brody's ex-sweetheart had moved back to Amarillo and wanted to meet up, and Tagger's long-time fiancée was putting pressure on him to set a date.

"My, my," Grace replied with a laugh, "between the two of you and Jarrod, this place is going to become nothing but old married men." She shot Mac a quick glance. "What about you, Palmer? What poor woman have you got holding on for an offering?"

Her blue eyes sparked with amusement, but he could see true curiosity there as well.

"Not a one. Interested?"

She blinked, her confidence by all appearances shattering…or maybe it was simply disgust.

Brody stopped mixing and stood up straight. "Well, that should do it. Are we ready to go?"

Tagger slapped him upside the arm. "Were you not paying attention? Mac here just proposed."

The redhead's brows pulled with confusion. "Proposed what?"

"To Grace, you idiot. Mac just proposed to Grace."

Brody looked their way, his mouth hanging open.

Snapping out of what had looked like a trance, Grace rolled her eyes. "That wasn't a proposal. It was a *mind-your-own-business*, and now we all better put our minds to our business. We have cattle to feed."

It was her way of running, and after opening

himself up so wide for public humiliation, he was more than willing to let her go.

He and Grace hopped in the front of the truck while Brody and Tagger hung on tight in back. Soon, they were nearing the pens.

"So, what are you going to do when the men start to marry?" She looked his way. "Will you bring out their wives?"

"It depends on them, really. Usually when ranch hands marry, they tend to move on." He looked up into his rearview mirror and back at the two men. "I imagine we've been lucky to keep them as long as we have. I certainly wouldn't mind keeping them longer. They're good men."

"We could always bring in some doublewides. Set up a playground. Make staying a viable option."

Mac nodded his head, not quite convinced. "They'd have to sell the women on it first. And you know as well as I do—that's not always easy."

"True, but they'll be able to sell it a whole lot easier if they can show them a home."

"You have a home here, Grace, a beautiful home. Are you sold?"

She turned around to stare out the window. "That's entirely different. I'm not in love with one of the ranch hands. My life, my future, is somewhere out there." Her gaze drifted out toward the horizon, and she sighed.

The thought made his insides turn. As much as she enjoyed the ranch, and he could now plainly see she still did, she remained determined to leave. He had a lot of work to do it seemed, and he needed to do it fast, before Todd Ryan or some other fast talker lured her away from right under his nose.

Chapter Eight

Sitting on her bed with her back against the headboard, Grace turned another page in the Renaissance romance she'd found in a small collection downstairs. The novel was interesting enough, but her mind kept wandering, replacing the book's hero with one a little less charming.

It seemed as though Mac was always interfering in her love life, even the make-believe kind that came direct from another's imagination to hers.

She closed her eyes and tried to refocus.

If only she could quit rethinking that morning outside the stables, when he'd wrapped his arm around her and treated her as though she were his. It had been nearly two weeks, and she still couldn't stop thinking about it.

The oddest part was that she wasn't even sure the two of them together was something she'd want. So, why couldn't she get that morning out of her head? Why did his words from their trip back from the Baxters' keep coming back with such heartwarming remembrance?

"You deserve better," he'd said. *"You deserve someone who'll love you beyond the point of any doubts. Someone who'll wake up every morning knowing he's the luckiest man alive."*

She couldn't quit imagining him as that someone.

How ridiculous was that? They were nothing alike. They were like cats and dogs, fire and ice, angels and demons...okay, that was going a bit too far. She was hardly an angel.

Part of the problem was that she no longer knew where they stood. They were no longer at war, nor were they exactly friends. She had no idea where to place him, so he stayed forever in the back of her mind, unclaimed and undefined. Yes, it was better than daggers, but unfortunately, a little more uncomfortable than silence.

There'd been polite hellos, nods, and fleeting smiles. There was also something different in the way he looked at her these days, something that...lingered.

She shook away the vision. It was probably nothing. She needed to let it go and let things progress however they progressed. Things weren't so bad. They had, after all, managed actual conversation over dinner the past few nights.

"Certainly progress," she assured herself before running her finger over the page and looking for anything that rang familiar.

Oh, yes, that's where she'd drifted off. The hero had just bent down to kiss the heroine.

A soft knock rapped against her bedroom door. "Grace?"

She lowered the book to her lap. *Was that—?*

"Grace, are you in there?"

Her heart skipped a beat. Excitement burst from a memory into the present. *Yes, it was!* She'd know that voice anywhere. *Jenny Palmer!*

"It's unlocked." Reaching to her nightstand, Grace grabbed her bookmark and marked her spot in the romance.

The door opened, and a kind, familiar smile emerged around its corner. "Hello there, pretty lady. It's about time you came home."

Swinging her legs off the bed, Grace jumped to her feet and ran to her friend. "Man, am I ever glad to see you."

Jenny, a thanks-to-Clairol, stunning blonde, wrapped her arms around Grace and squeezed her tight. "Four long years," she said, in way of reprimand. "If I'd have known you and your grandmother were planning to stay gone so long, I'd have locked you both in your rooms. Shame on you for leaving me here alone with all these hooligans."

Grace leaned back and forced a look of concern. She knew full-well Jenny loved each and every one of the *hooligans* who lived at the ranch. "Have they been giving you a hard time?"

"Oh, you know how it is." Letting her go, she gave her a wink. "Those cowboys are never happy unless they're dishing it out right and left. They were born to stir up trouble. That grandfather of yours is the absolute worst. Let me tell you, there's nothing like a grizzly who feels he's been wronged."

Grace grimaced. "He's been a real bear, huh?"

"Was, the first year. A few temper tantrums, a lot of sulking, but I believe he's emerged a humbled man. He misses her, Grace, something awful. Do you think she'll ever come back?"

"Um…" She hesitated, ashamed of the role she may have played. "I think I better call her and retract a few theories I may have inadvertently laid about life…love…men."

It was Jenny's turn to grimace, but she countered it quickly with an understanding nod. "I see."

"Yeah." She shifted her weight, ran a hand nervously up her arm. "I probably haven't been the most positive influence these past few years. My pep-talks haven't exactly been...well, peppy."

Mac's mother took a step back, a slightly sad and troubled expression pulling gently at her brows. "I've been so worried about you. I should have called. I should have talked to you about what happened." She gave a regretful shake of her head. "In truth, I simply didn't know what to say. I wasn't even sure if you'd want to talk to me. But I should have reached out. I should have tried harder than the occasional letter and random postcard."

Grace had always known why the call never came, and she'd been more than a little thankful it hadn't. What, after all, was there to say?

"It's all right." She offered her forgiveness with a genuine smile. "It wasn't anything anyone could help me through. I had to do it on my own. I'm kind of like my grandfather—I threw a few fits, did a lot of sulking, and emerged, hopefully, a better person." She shrugged. "Definitely a stronger person."

Jenny gave her a blatant once-over. "You do look well. In fact, you look amazing, even prettier than the day you left. And Lord knows, I would have sworn that impossible."

She smiled. "You always were the flatterer."

"Maybe so, but it's still true." Jenny watched her silently a few seconds before nodding. "I worried about you, but I always knew you'd be all right. You're a fighter, Grace Wade, just like your grandfather, only slightly less cantankerous."

"Slightly less?"

The motherly blonde laughed but never recanted. "There's someone I'd like you to meet," she said, taking Grace's hands in hers. "Someone very special to my heart."

"Doc? I know Doc."

"That man…" Jenny shook her head and grinned. "He's a keeper, let me tell you. But, no, this is someone else. Will you come with me?"

With such excitement in her friend's voice, how could she refuse? And so she found herself, only a few short minutes later, following the older woman into the barn.

"Gently," she heard Mac warn from the far corner.

Sweet baby squeals and giggles erupted directly after.

Grace's heart jumped as if capturing the sounds. Then it stopped, as did she, dead in her tracks. Her whole body went stiff, like she'd been doused in plaster, her legs simply refusing to move.

Oh, no! She had to work to hold back the cry that exploded from her chest and roared to her mind.

More squeals. A few gurgles and coos.

Her heart wasn't beating, but her adrenaline was racing. *No. No. No! I'm not ready.*

Jenny grabbed her hand, and Grace nearly jumped through the hayloft.

"Please," her friend said, patting her hand between her own. "It's only Ellie."

Only Ellie. No Garrett. No Jackie. Just a small child she was every bit as terrified to meet. Her stomach turned, introducing the urge for her to do the same. Turn and run fast, very fast, as fast and as far away as she could.

The child's shrills and gurgles were reaching out to grab old dreams purposefully shelved, but knocking free, like dust, old feelings left unvisited through years of avoidance.

Looking back toward the corner, Grace literally shook. This would have been her life, was *supposed to* have been her world—her ranch, her baby, her dream.

"You can do this," Jenny encouraged.

She found herself walking forward, but in her heart, she'd already turned and ran far away. She'd go through the motions, fake pleasantries and then follow her heart as far as it needed to run.

They rounded the post separating the small area where the mother and pups were kept. Sitting on one of the bales of hay surrounding the puppies was Mac. His back was to her, but Grace could tell he held in his hands a bouncing armful of excitement.

"Mac," Jenny announced their arrival.

Standing, he lifted the little girl into his arms and turned their way, his eyes widening a fraction as he spotted her.

"Grace," Jenny said, "I'd like you to meet Eleisha Rose Palmer. We all call her Ellie."

Curious black eyes looked her way from a full and adorable face. The little girl smiled and bounced in Mac's arms.

Grace's vision blurred through the tears that welled in her eyes. Her throat tried to close. She forced it open with a swallow. "She's precious."

And she was. Dark hair like her mother's curled in large wisps like her uncle's. Round, perfectly pink cheeks highlighted a face that would one day slim, leaving behind a beautiful young girl.

She cooed and pointed back to the puppies, offering Grace a peek at her find.

An unexpected warmth spread from her heart clear through the whole of her body. The shaking stopped and instinct kicked in. She moved closer, looking over the little girl's shoulder toward the bundles of fur. "Have you found yourself some new friends?"

Ellie cooed some more in way of explanation.

"They're wonderful, aren't they?"

A bright smile said even more than words could have relayed. Ellie reached out her arms, asking to be taken.

Hesitating, Grace looked first to Jenny then to Mac.

"I'd tell you she doesn't bite," Mac said before kissing his niece on her rosy little cheek, "but that wouldn't give fair notice. She has two new chompers and often attacks without warning."

Jenny laughed. "She's simply trying to bite the ornery out of you. She's too young yet to know some things are too solid."

Grace held out her arms, and Ellie leaned right in, giggling with excitement as she was taken and then promptly rubbing her nose against Grace's shirt, surely a sign of bonding. Her heart melted clear to thawed. Together, they sat on the stack Mac had only seconds ago vacated.

Two pups were still busy feeding on their mom, but Mac's chubby pup and two of his littermates played beside the edge. With her free hand, Grace reached down and scooped out Mac's future best friend.

"Careful," he warned. "Ellie doesn't really understand gentle."

The puppy sniffed at the child's small toes. Ellie pulled in her feet. Leaning forward, she laughed with sheer delight.

In very short time, Grace and the little girl became good friends. So much so, she was sad to see her go when Jenny picked her up and they headed out to make lunch.

"She's wonderful." Grace cuddled the puppy then placed him back with his litter before standing.

"Yeah." Mac watched his mother and niece make their way across the yard. "She's pretty great."

Images of him and the child played in her head. Trying to stifle a giggle, she looked down to her feet. She felt his gaze upon her, but wasn't brave enough to acknowledge it.

"What's tickled your toes?" he asked, following her gaze to the hay at her feet.

"I just," she began, but had to stop to fight her amusement. "I never would have imagined you talking baby talk." She looked up, bit at her lip, and then, unable to contain it, she snickered.

An instant scowl appeared between his brows. "I most definitely did not."

"Oh," she said on a rumble of laughter, "you most definitely did."

His arms crossed over his chest.

Noting his disfavor, she covered her mouth with her hand and laughed behind its cover.

His eyes may have narrowed, but it was amusement they now hid. "I can still see you're laughing."

Her shoulders shook. "No, I'm not."

Taking a menacing step toward her, he wrapped his hand around her wrist and pulled away her hand. "Yes, you are."

"Is that a puppy?" she mimicked his coo then once again laughed out loud, this time blatantly and without remorse.

Still holding firm to her wrist, he took another step closer.

Her gaze locked with his as the air swarmed with a new kind of energy—sharp, intense, very much aware. She sensed the change, and her pulse raced with excitement, but still the laughter came.

Like a cat thrilled with the game, she batted at her prey. "Maybe if you talked that sweet to Last Ride, he'd let you stay on."

Amusement lifted the corners of his mouth into a heart-stopping grin. Mischief flashed in his eyes. He looked daunting, tempting, and as sexy as any cowboy ever had. Tilting his head, his gaze fell to her lips.

At that moment, she wanted nothing more than to take hold of his curls and pull him down to where his mouth could take over what his gaze had clearly started.

Even without her assistance, he moved in closer. "If I talked that kind of sweet talk to Last Ride, I think he'd probably give me a beating."

The warmth of his breath brushed lightly against her skin. Arousal flared fast and furious. It hit her like one gigantic wave forged low beneath her surface and built solely to engulf her. So powerful, she wondered if he hadn't felt it, too.

The way he was looking at her suggested maybe he had.

"A beating as opposed to what? Giving you a hurl?" She hardly recognized her own voice—low and slightly raspy.

He laughed and looked away, yet stayed where he stood. "Actually, he's been given the pleasure of giving me both now once. I'm not particularly eager to give him another go."

"You were hurt?"

He studied her quietly a moment. "Is that glee or concern? I couldn't quite tell."

She hesitated. Easy banter between them was new. She didn't want to do anything that might chase it away. "I wouldn't want to see you hurt."

He grinned. "But hurled is okay?"

Smiling, she looked down. "Don't ask me to be nice."

He reached out and tenderly ran the back of his hand down her cheek. "Nice is no fun."

Her flesh warmed beneath his touch, and her breathing quickened. She trembled. Wise or foolish, if she could have stopped that moment in time, she would have.

The sound of boots hurrying across dirt broke into the moment. "Mac?" Phil called into the barn.

Mac's lids lowered. He stiffened and cursed under his breath, at no time attempting to hide from her his disappointment. "Over here," he hollered back, slowly stepping away from her and out into the open. He turned toward the barn door. "What's up?"

"We're heading out to fix that fence near Round Creek. You comin' or are you staying behind to play with the puppies?" Phil snickered, but his chuckles disappeared as Grace moved around the post to stand beside Mac.

"Oh!" The foreman startled and took off his Stetson to hold out in front of him. "Evening, Grace. I..." He shuffled his feet. "I ahh...didn't see ya...standing there."

She nodded his way. "Phil."

The older man pursed his lips and stood silently sizing up the situation. By the look on his face, she'd say he'd put two and two together and come up with five.

She was right.

"We've got this, boss." He shifted his hat nervously from one hand to the other. "No need to leave things here. They probably need your attention more than any fence. You stay and take care of...ah...things."

"Real smooth, Phil." Mac shook his head and stepped across the barn to grab his hat off the hood of the old truck that was back inside for a new set of repairs. He brushed the Stetson off against his jeans and grinned her way. "I imagine *things* here can wait."

What? Grace stared at the roguish cowboy incredulously. What was he thinking?

The insinuation was blatant. If she didn't correct the idea, and correct it quickly, the entire ranch would soon be thinking she and Mac were having some kind of *thing*. The men here had numerous good qualities, tact wasn't one of them. She had to set the foreman straight.

"Actually, Phil, you didn't interrupt a thing."

The pleased, though uncomfortable, look on his face suggested he wasn't buying it. What she needed was a distraction—something to occupy his mind before he filled the minds of the others with ideas of a romantic tryst between her and *the boss*.

"Mac and I were just talking about the last bull rides," she blurted, grasping at the first thought that came to mind.

Mac's hat froze halfway to his head. He sent a curious stare her way but didn't say a word.

"Yeah?" Phil eagerly picked up the change in topic. "They were some impressive rides, weren't they?"

"Sure were." She laughed nervously. "In fact, that's exactly what we were saying."

The sexy cowboy's lids narrowed as he leaned back against the truck. "It was?"

"Of course it was," she insisted between gritted teeth.

"Interesting." He crossed one ankle over the other. "I guess I forgot that part. All I remember was some…" He paused, smiled shamelessly, and added, "sweet talk."

What! Grace choked as she tried to swallow the lump that caught in her throat. A coughing fit pursued.

"You all right, Grace?" Mac took a step in her direction, but she pointed him back to the truck.

Why was he purposefully making things so difficult? He knew his men. He should know there'd be repercussions.

Her head spun with frustration. What could she do? She needed his cooperation, and she needed it now.

A desperate idea flashed in her head as the coughing stopped. She moved the pointed finger high into the air. "That's right." She delivered the same shameless smile right back to him. "We were planning a strategy to sweet talk a bull." She turned her full attention to Phil. "Mac was telling me how he'd like another go at Last Ride."

"Last Ride?" Phil's brow rose high as he shot a surprised glance to Mac.

Lids narrowed once again, but not before the spark of battle flashed vividly from behind steely blue eyes. Back to leaning against the pickup, he crossed his arms over his chest, a casual gesture that felt suspiciously like a threat.

Unease rang a warning bell, but stubbornness still lifted her chin. "That's right," she continued. "He feels he's been bettered. He wants another go."

"Is that right?" Phil's weathered hand rubbed at the back of his neck. "Well, that is interesting."

"Isn't it?" Mac's voice came a little deeper than normal and potently sexy with its strongly pronounced, yet insanely relaxed, Texas drawl. He moistened his lips then smiled a smile so menacing it would have given pause to the devil himself. "Do you know what makes it even more interesting?"

Grace's stomach turned, as did her smile.

The foreman's face lit with anticipation. "What's that, boss?"

"The wager we made attached to it."

"Wager?" Grace repeated, a chill forming from inside. He was looking far too pleased with himself, and that couldn't possibly bode well for her.

This time, the shudder that ran through her was anything but pleasant.

"You're going to appreciate this one, Phil." Poised in his nonchalant fashion, like he hadn't a care in all the world, Mac laid down his retaliation. "It was Grace's idea, of course. And like all her ideas," he said with a wink in her direction, "it's a clever one."

Clenching her palms nervously, their moisture dampening the tips of her fingers, she was almost certain she heard doom chuckling from the rafters. Perhaps she'd saved face, but she had a feeling she was soon to lose her backbone.

"Don't leave me in suspense," Phil encouraged. By all appearances, he was actually buying the long string of bull.

Mac, reveling in her discomfort, grinned. "If I ride the beast the full count, Grace here becomes my servant for an entire day, bowing, of course, to my every whim."

Her mouth dropped.

Phil scowled, shifting his weight from one leg to the other. "Sounds a bit risky."

"All things *G* rated, of course," he added for good show. "Unless, of course, Grace wants to up the ante."

A gasp escaped her open mouth.

"But then again," he hesitated, drawing out the moment to give it a silent sort of drum roll. "It's possible you've changed your mind and now wish to back down? I'm a gentleman. I'll allow it."

Oh, wouldn't he just.

Her fingers tapped against the sides of her jeans. If only she could think of a way to wipe that smug and sure grin right off his face.

"Gracie's made of stronger stuff than that," the amused foreman assured. "She ain't backing down, are you, sweetheart?"

Well, when put like that...

"So, what does she get if you don't ride the count?"

Grace perked up. She'd forgotten entirely about the flip side of the coin. "Good question, Phil." Wrapping her arms, one over the other, she shifted her weight to look in Mac's direction. "What *does* happen if you don't last the eight? What do *I* get?"

Raising a brow as though the idea preposterous, he lifted high an open palm in her direction. "Name it."

"Name it?" she repeated, suspecting the terms too good to be true.

"Absolutely. Anything. Well, close anyway. Money and pride are the only limits. If you want me to do your chores for a day, I'll do them. Want me to polish your nails? Not a problem. If you'd like me to massage your back while reading poetry, I won't promise a remarkable delivery, but I'll promise you a gallant effort."

A brilliant idea flashed. Knowing how much it would serve to annoy him, it made her nearly giddy with excitement. "I have your word on that?" She tried her best to act indifferent, fearing if he saw how much she now wanted it, he'd change his mind and back out.

"You do." He drew an X across his heart with his finger. "And, sweetheart," he added with a downright wicked grin. "I won't even limit you with a rating restriction."

Finding his grin contagious, she lost her struggle and smiled wide. "Very generous."

"I'm good with naughty," he explained, wiggling his brows.

"I'll keep that in mind." She tried to act appalled, but in truth, she was finding his scoundrel side a little too charming. It was time to put an end to it all.

Sorry, Mr. Palmer, but this hand is mine.

"All right, Mac, you have yourself a deal."

Phil threw back his head and roared with laughter. "Wait 'til the men hear about this." He put his hat back on and headed out the door.

"Like taking candy from a baby," Mac said, still leaning against the truck as pleased as could be. "I hope you've at least learned your lesson."

Moistening her lips, she nodded. "Feeling pretty good about yourself, are you?"

He shrugged his shoulders. "A day of pampering, a pretty little lady to run after my every whim—yeah, I'm feeling all right."

"Just so you pay up when you lose, because *this baby* has her mind set on one particularly sweet piece of candy."

He uncrossed his ankles and pushed himself away from the truck. "And what sweet little piece of candy is that, do tell?"

"Oh…a cute little blue book, I like to call my passport."

Shit! Mac's lip twitched at the very tip of what he now realized had been an overly-confident grin. He'd walked straight into her web with his cowboy boots strutting. "Now, wait a minute—"

"Name it," she repeated his words with a wide-eyed, innocent stare. "Isn't that what you said?"

"Well, yes, but—"

"But?" Pursing her lips, she batted her lashes, mocking him in a way easily recognized but not so easily chastised.

His insides knotted. He should really let the woman go. She was likely to leave him with ulcers. With an exaggerated sigh, he leaned forward, dropped his head into his hands, and gazed down at the dirt floor. It had been a long while since he'd been bettered.

Curse his boastful pride. He liked having her passport. It assured him she wouldn't simply disappear without him knowing, without him having an opportunity to somehow intervene. And he would definitely intervene the next time…if given the chance.

The strides of her boots against the barn's floor gave him warning she was coming, but still, it surprised him when he suddenly found her staring up at him from beside his bent knees. Her lips were pursed, her expression torn. If he didn't know her better, he may have assumed her truly concerned.

"Problems?" Her voice was dripping with sweetness.

His biggest problem at the moment was a fierce desire starting to swell not far from where she leaned. He had a real notion to pull her into his arms and make love to her there and then…probably not a problem he ought to share.

"I hadn't considered the passport," he confessed.

"Shame." She straightened to full height. "Would it have made a difference?"

He followed her up to standing. "You know it would have. Otherwise, you wouldn't have waited to name it nor taken such immense satisfaction in doing so."

"Really?" She tilted her head, looking at him as though he were sad. "You would have let a tiny little booklet hold you back?"

It was a coax and obvious, as obvious as the pleasure she was taking from her win. *Lord, have mercy, the woman is every kind of temptation.*

"I wouldn't have backed out. I'd have made another exception."

"Is that so?" She shifted her weight against one leg and lifted a brow in curious fashion. "It means that much to you—having that power?"

"You need to stick it out, Grace. I think you know that as much as I do."

She reached out with mock sympathy and patted his shoulder. "I'm not planning on using it right away if that's what has you worried."

He looked up toward the rafters and laughed, finally finding the humor in the hole he had dug himself. "Has anyone ever told you what an aggravating woman you are?"

Her smile looked anything but worried. "You're only sore because I've bettered you, and for the record, I think you want my passport because you'd miss me." She was only teasing, he knew, because she had no idea she'd just nailed the tail on the donkey.

In one quick move, he stepped forward and turned to stand in front of her, forcing her to take a step back as he reached out his arms, boxing her in against the truck. "You haven't won yet, and on the very real chance that you don't, it might serve you better to play it a little less smug."

"You have a point," she acknowledged, but her beautiful smile never faltered—not exactly the vision of a woman repentant.

He wondered if she truly was that confident he wouldn't make it, or simply confident that if he did, she could handle whatever he dished out. Both seemed a challenge he wouldn't want to fail.

Unable to resist the temptation, he leaned a little

closer to her lips. "If you're not going to use the passport, why do you want it so badly?"

She swallowed, her mouth slightly parting as she took a shaky breath. "I've already told you. It's mine. I want it back. It's that simple."

Nothing that had anything to do with Grace Wade was ever simple.

"All right, Grace. If I fail to stay the count, the little blue book is yours." Leaning in closer, he dropped his volume to a husky low. "But I'm staying the count, and when I do, you and I might very well be roasting marshmallows over its ashes."

Her lips quivered slightly. Though it was impossible to say for certain, he'd almost swear she leaned in closer. "I could always put in for another."

"Yes, but that would take time, not to mention a flight into Amarillo...and guess who's the pilot?"

"Brody can fly."

"Brody would need my plane."

Wrinkling her adorable nose, she closed her eyes. "I hadn't thought of that." She stood there silently a moment, seemingly regretful. But in the very next moment, she opened her eyes and grinned. "Good thing you'll never make the count."

Mac couldn't help the answering grin. The woman had the audacity of a prize fighter. It was one in a million things he found irresistible about her.

"Boss, you coming?" Brody hollered into the barn.

His buddies were sure doing a good job of picking bad timing. He should have taken Phil up on his offer and let them go it alone.

"Coming," he yelled back over his shoulder, unable to look away from the sparkle in her eyes and the lovely tilt of her lips.

She'd changed over the last few weeks, slowly letting her guard down until the real woman could now be seen clearly beneath. And she was everything he'd sensed for so long and more—fun, witty, hot to the core. One day, and it wouldn't be long in coming, he was going to give her the kiss her eyes said she wanted.

He pushed himself away from the truck and the blue-eyed temptress against it. "We'll likely be late. Will you let Eldon know?"

She looked down with what he could only hope was disappointment. "I'll tell him."

****

The screen door squeaked open then danced a slow stop-and-go as it made its way back to closed.

"Hey there, pretty lady, mind a passenger?" her grandfather asked.

Scooting over on the front-porch swing, Grace tapped the seat beside her. "Share my swing with a handsome devil like yourself? I'd be honored."

Quiet times with her grandfather had been rare through the years, mostly because for years he'd put in such long hours working on the ranch. It had been nice, over the last few weeks, to have him so often to herself, to finally get to know and understand a little better the man who had, for so long, been somewhat of an enigma.

He sat, wrapping his arm around the back of the swing as he followed her gaze out toward the horizon. As was typical for that time of year, there was a spectacular sunset sitting in vibrant hues of orange high in the sky. It fell toward the earth in tiers of lightening shades, eventually vanishing behind the distant hills.

"Beautiful, isn't it?" Taking in a deep breath, her grandfather then slowly let it out. He nodded toward the sky. "I would miss this perhaps the most. I love the sunset here. How many men are lucky enough to have a touch of heaven right outside their door?"

As her feet, following the swing's easy glide, brushed back across the wood of the veranda's floor, she smiled. Her grandfather had found his dream and lived his life to its fullest. No matter what the future held, she would always be glad she'd gotten to share a bit of that dream with him.

She leaned her head against his shoulder. "I wish everything in life could be this beautiful, this simple."

He gave her a healthy squeeze. "I think *too easy* dulls our senses. We need the tough to truly appreciate moments like this." He chuckled lightly. "I imagine that's why life chooses to throw us the occasional curve ball."

She couldn't help but wonder if *his* curve ball had been her grandmother leaving.

For years, her grandparents had fought the same fight—he'd broken his promise. To get her grandmother to leave her home and replant in Texas, he'd promised her the occasional trip back home as well as vacations to see their son and his wife at their many excavation sites. But season after season and year after year, duties at the ranch had prevented them from leaving.

"Excuses," her grandmother had called them. "The boys," she had pointed out frequently, "were more than capable of taking care of the ranch for a month's time or better."

Gramps had been stubborn, typically ending the

fights by saying he didn't have time to bicker about such things and then storming out of the house. Her grandmother had always let the matter drop, hoping the next season would bring another opportunity.

But it never did…until four years back, when Grace had returned to the ranch broken and desperate.

For the first time in her life, she, too, had wanted as far away from the ranch as she could possibly get. Her grandmother had jumped at the chance to return home for a while. *"Gracie needs this,"* she'd told her husband. Then, along with Grace, she'd struck a deal. Four years of education for two years of work back at the ranch. And to make sure their granddaughter got safely settled in and ready for life on her own, Grams would spend the first year in Vancouver with her.

Her grandfather had first balked at the idea. But when his wife reminded him of his broken promise, he'd caved. That's how it had started. Insecurities and stubborn wills later introduced some alterations to the plan.

Grace stared down to her grandfather's aging hands. It had to end. Tomorrow, she'd try once again to get hold of her grandmother. She needed to know exactly what she was thinking and if there was a chance she'd ever return.

In the distance, cows mooed as a frog croaked for his sweetheart somewhere out in the yard. The scents of hay and bush laid claim to the dusk as the slightest breeze fought to cool the lingering heat. She embraced it all, remembering too easily why she'd lost her heart to the ranch.

Gently swinging back and forth, she and Gramps watched the sky darken and the colors fade.

"I hear you've made yourself a little wager," he eventually said, pulling her back from memories she'd be better off to forget.

She cast him a quick glance, expecting disapproval but not finding it. "Boy, news sure travels fast around these parts."

"It doesn't have far to travel." Her grandfather nodded toward the veranda's railing. "I was out here earlier when I saw Phil hurrying out of the barn looking like the cat who'd just swallowed the canary. I called him over, and he gave me the lowdown." He shook his head and grinned. "Are you sure you know what it is you're asking for, Grace Elizabeth?"

She nudged his shoulder affectionately. "Don't worry, Grandpa, this one borders on a 'sure thing.'"

Snorting a laugh, he shook his head. "You obviously don't know the man."

"Perhaps you haven't seen the bull. It's a wonder anyone's ridden him. That is one mighty piece of dirt-stomping ornery."

"A description that could as comfortably fit the cowboy as it fits the bull. I doubt this is as sure as you believe. Mac knows how to ride. I imagine he'll ride even better to prove a point."

She let her head drop back against his arm as she moaned. "That would be my luck."

He squeezed her shoulder. "Speaking of luck, what evil deeds have you in mind for him if he doesn't make the count? I have to assume you're after his pride."

She pretended to be appalled. "I simply want him to give me back something that is already mine."

"And what's that?"

"My passport."

"Your passport?" He leaned up only to stare back at her. "What's Mac doing with your passport?"

"Sticking his nose where it doesn't belong."

He continued to stare for a long, thoughtful moment. She had the unnerving feeling he was seeing straight through her, and apparently he was.

"Maybe...or maybe he's making sure your nose stays where it ought."

She shrugged and looked away.

Her grandfather leaned back against the swing. "I'll have to watch this ride, I reckon."

"Have you ever ridden a bull, Grandpa?"

"One, and one was lesson enough. 'Bout broke my neck as well as my pride. Those beasts aren't gentle on their calm days."

"You...you don't imagine Mac could be hurt?" It was a thought that had dawned on her earlier, but not until several minutes after the ridiculous deal had already been struck.

"Getting hurt is always a risk, but not one that's ever stopped one of these roughnecks. They're too young to care that the spills of today are their pains of tomorrow. It's a truth that tends to hit us all several years too late."

She flinched. "Maybe you should talk him out of it."

Gramps' brows lifted high in surprise. "There's been very little I've ever talked that lad into or out of. If you don't want him to ride, tell him yourself. Though, he'll probably figure you're merely running scared."

It was her turn to snort a laugh. "I'm not scared."

"And neither is he. Ever hear the one about the two stubborn goats who tried to cross the road?"

She blinked. "What?"

"Maybe it was mules. Oh, never mind. I never could remember the punchline anyhow. But my point is, if you're worried about him, tell him. Even if he still rides, at least he knows you care."

"Oh, Grandpa, Mac Palmer has never cared about my opinion of him."

"Is that so?" He eyed her doubtfully. "Last I'd heard, Mac had already made his last try on Last Ride. I wonder what changed his mind."

He had a point, one that left her feeling ever so slightly more responsible. Why *would* Mac suddenly care what she thought? Most likely, it was some macho thing.

Crap! She'd bullied him into some macho thing.

Her shoulders fell. "I'll talk to him."

"That's my girl." Her grandfather, once again, patted her shoulder. Then, pursing his lips, he seemed to be mulling something over.

She raised her brows. "Is there something else I should do?"

He shook his head and scratched at the back of his neck, a nervous habit she recognized immediately.

"Grandpa, what is it?"

"There's something you need to know."

"Okay."

"Garrett and Jackie are flying in tomorrow to pick up Miss Ellie."

Her heart suddenly felt as though it were pumping molasses, every organ seemed to slow as sweat broke out from pores she didn't even know existed.

Now she was scared.

Why hadn't it dawned on her? Of course they were

coming. Jenny and Doc had had their pilot stop by Garrett's ranch on their way back from Wichita, but that pilot was long gone. Grace should have realized it would be Garrett picking up his child. He certainly wasn't going to leave his daughter there forever.

Oddly enough, her thoughts had never quite made it through the particulars. She'd been so wrapped up in Mac and the events of the afternoon that she'd missed the obvious and failed to give the situation its proper dose of dread. She definitely dreaded it now. Ellie was a doll and easy to love…her parents were an entirely different matter.

"Don't worry, Grandpa. I won't make a scene. In fact, I'll make myself scarce. Believe me. I have no problem playing invisible."

He scowled. "Why would you want to hide? You've done nothing wrong." He shifted in the swing to face her directly. "Look, honey, this is a ride I want you to take like the champ you are. It's time to mend fences."

"That's sweet, Grandpa, and I love you for it, but…" But no matter what she thought of Garrett now, the humiliation and hurt were still very much real.

Her grandfather's eyes seemed to soften. He took another deep breath. "There's something else I need to talk to you about."

"You're telling me there's more?"

Gramps took her hand and held it gently between his. "A while back, I said something I feel needs clarified."

Instantly, she began searching her memory. There'd been a few digs. He didn't particularly care for her floral-scented perfume, and one of her tousled, hair-in-a-bun styles offended his sense of grooming. He'd said it reminded him of a scarecrow his parents use to have on their farm. He'd also suggested her driving could use some improving…

Of course, he said clarified not apologized for, and when was the last time Eldon Wade had apologized for anything? No, it was probably some rude comment he'd made about her grandmother.

Wait a minute! That was odd. Looking back, she realized he hadn't made a single snide comment about her grandmother since that first day on the porch.

She shot him a curious glance out the corner of her eye. "What is it, Grandpa?"

"Before you and Mac left for the Baxter's to pick up those quads…" He paused as though finding it difficult. "I made a really stupid comment about Garrett's marrying you being a mistake."

Her heart still fell slightly with the words. Looking down toward their joined hands, she shrugged a shoulder. "It's all right, Grandpa. It's probably true."

"Grace Elizabeth Wade, you are *no one's* mistake. You are a fine woman, a truly worthy soul. Any man, and I do mean *any* man, would be lucky to have you. Most would not be worthy." He took a deep breath and let it out slowly. "That being said, I do believe marriage to Garrett Palmer would have been a mistake, and I mean a mistake for both of you. It was not hard to see there was no spark between you. I do believe he loved you, and I do believe you felt the same for him. You two, very well, may have had a long and respectful marriage."

His point was suddenly a little less clear. She lifted her head, eying him curiously. "And that would be a bad thing?"

"I can't imagine anything more boring." He wrinkled his nose as though he'd tasted something vile.

She laughed. "Grandpa, you and grandma had a long, and for many years, respectful marriage."

"Your grandmother and I have had a long and loving marriage, but there were also sparks, plenty of sparks, be they of passion or the clashing of wills. I wouldn't trade the years I've had with your grandmother for a hundred more years of life. That's the kind of love I want for you, not some mild, dull, repetitive existence. Garrett's a wonderful man. You're a wonderful woman. But you were a bloody awful pairing. Marrying each other would have been a terrible mistake, and that is no reflection on either of you."

It was a conclusion she'd already come to, though perhaps a slight bit less gracefully. She smiled, turning her hands to squeeze those which held hers. "Thanks, Grandpa. It means a lot to me."

"And you mean the world to me. I probably haven't said that enough."

"Maybe not with words." Leaning forward, she kissed his wrinkled brow. "I love you, too, Grandpa."

****

Hearing the front door close, Grace put down the mug she'd been drying to hurry out of the kitchen and quickly down the unlit hall. She was determined, before the situation got any further out of control, to put an end to the ride she herself had instigated.

"Oh!" she shrieked as she collided full-force with a dark form at the bottom of the steps.

"Hey!" Mac straightened from his bent position. His expression, lit vaguely by the distant kitchen light, shifted from startled to pleased. "Sweetheart, what's the hurry?" His arms wrapped around her as she steadied herself against his chest. He looked down to her hands gripping his shirt, and his smile grew. "What is this, Grace? Are you excited to see me?"

The truth was, it felt wonderful there in his arms, in that split second before awkwardness caught up with reality. Her flesh, where they touched, tingled with delight. In fact, her senses were practically applauding their approval. *Yes. The answer is yes!* But she wouldn't be sharing that soon, and soon enough, the awkwardness descended.

Still wrapped in his arms and feeling plenty foolish, she stared at him in surprise. "What were you thinking, springing up at me out of nowhere?"

"It was hardly my intention to *spring up* on anyone." He nodded down toward the rug sitting to the side of the steps—the one where all good cowpokes left their soiled boots. "It's you who sprang out of nowhere. What are you doing sprinting down the hall in the dark?"

He probably had a point. She forced a smile. "Sorry. I was hoping to catch you." She tried to push away.

His arms wrapped a little tighter. "It seems I've turned the tables. That's what you get for not planning your attacks a bit more carefully."

Grace eyed the arms still holding her captive. "Noted. Thanks for the catch by the way."

"My pleasure. What were you planning to do with me once you caught me?" His somewhat unsettling smile shifted to more of an ominous grin. He bent closer and whispered, "If you have the right answer, I might hand myself over."

Her heart skipped a beat as her body warmed in all the wrong places. An urge, nearly overwhelming, encouraged her to wrap her limbs around him. Thankfully her wits, on full alert, waged war against the impulse. "You can probably let me go now."

There was a definite hesitation, but he did eventually release her. "You were looking for me?"

"Yes, actually for a couple of reasons. First, there's a plate for you inside the oven. It's roasted chicken and mashed potatoes…oh, and carrots," she added with a little too much excitement.

His brows lifted. He smiled. "Sounds great. Thanks. And the second reason?"

Biting nervously into her lip, she grimaced.

"This ought to be good," he said, taking off his hat and placing it over the post at the bottom of the steps.

Wringing her hands together, she wished she'd given her plea more thought. It had sounded pretty good when she rehearsed it earlier; but now, with this ever-so-unnerving audience, it seemed a little weak. "I was talking to Grandfather earlier, you see, and I…" She stopped to clear her throat…and maybe to gain a better grip on her nerve. "Well, I was thinking, upon reflection—"

His brow pulled. "Grace, spit it out."

"I was hoping to talk some sense into you."

"I was right," he said, his eyes narrowing in on the limbs still wringing circles. "This is going to be good."

Unclenching her hands, she pushed one inside the front pocket of her jeans and pulled out a well-folded piece of paper. "Did you know the number of injuries to bull riders each year is staggering?"

They both looked down to where she hurriedly worked her fingers to open up the facts. "I did a little research tonight online." She paused, glancing toward the light switch. "Wait here a second. I'll turn on the light."

He pulled the paper out of her hands. "I'm aware of the dangers, Grace. It's not a safe sport. That's the fun of it."

"Fun?" she threw back the adjective. "What's so fun about getting your skull bashed in or your jewels trampled?"

Despite the surrounding darkness, his eyes still managed to glisten with amusement. "You worried about my jewels, Grace?"

Her lips lifted with amusement despite her best efforts to ignore his bad behavior. "That's not my point."

"Oh," he said, clicking his tongue as he nodded his head, "I believe it is."

"I've a proposition for you."

Those steel-blue eyes managed to shine even brighter. His right brow rose to an arch. "Well, this just gets better and better. Sorry for the interruption. Please, Grace, continue."

In this mood, the man proved simply irresistible, an odd mix of naughty and nice, though she'd wager at that moment it was the naughty that had hold of his tail. That shameless smile, brimming to the rim with deviltry, had to have been brewed in a very warm pot.

Once again, she cleared her throat, trying her best to collect her tumbling thoughts. It was hard to focus on anything with him standing so close and with his demeanor so teasing.

"Could you possibly be serious?"

"I am." He looked anything but. "I seriously want to hear your proposition."

The man could distract a striking cobra.

She sighed. "Please, Mac, I want you to take what I have to say seriously. This is very important."

Tilting his head ever so slightly, he narrowed his gaze and studied her stoic expression. "All right, you have my attention."

"I don't want you to ride Last Ride."

"I figured that was where this was going. What's wrong? Are you afraid of what I'll have you do?"

His gaze dropped to her lips, and instantly her thoughts wandered back to the barn and the kiss that never was. It was a memory that easily came to mind, as she'd already been playing it over and over in her head. What if their lips had met? What if—

"Grace?"

"Yes?"

"Yes, you're afraid?"

She blinked then tried to replay their discussion, giving herself a mental slap for drifting. "No. Well, yes, but not for me, for you. I'm afraid for you."

"Why the sudden concern?"

Grace searched his face—his intense gaze, his taut lips, the stubborn tilt of his jaw. Convincing him wouldn't be easy. She then glanced toward the stairs. Her grandfather had retired earlier to his room. If he was already sleeping, she didn't want to wake him. "Let's talk in the living room." She headed that way.

Mac followed right behind her.

"It's hardly sudden," she said, looking his way over her shoulder. "It's actually more like delayed.

Concern for your wellbeing should have always come first."

"First before what—the setup?"

Stopping in the middle of the room, she turned back to face him. "Yes."

He was closer to her than she'd realized. Not even a step separated them. Reaching out, he grabbed a handful of her hair only to watch it slide through his fingers. "Why did you do it?"

She swallowed, surprised by his action and the warmth in his eyes. "Distraction. Retaliation."

He looked away from his hand and into her eyes, obviously lost as to what she was getting at.

"I didn't want Phil thinking there was something going on between us. So, I threw out the first stupid thing that came to mind." Guilt settled as a throb at the back of her throat. She closed her eyes and shook her head. "Stupid. It was a stupid thing to do, and a bad place to put you."

"Is it really such a terrible thought—the two of us together?"

She stared at him dumbfounded. What exactly was he after? Certainly, he couldn't be hurt. After pushing her away for years, there wasn't a chance it was something he wanted, not really, not long term, and long term was the only thing a wise man would ever introduce to his crew.

Looking down toward the ground, she stammered, "It's not a terrible thought. It's a wrong thought. We're not together. We're not *a thing*. We're more…well, we're more…" What were they? No longer enemies, could they now be called friends? Maybe, but it was different from any friendship she'd ever had. Her friends didn't make her tingle, anticipate, giddy. Her friends didn't drive her so completely insane.

"It's all right, Grace. You don't have to define it. I know there's a lot of history behind us."

"Exactly, and there's also my history with Garrett. I just don't want the men to think…" How could she put it without sounding too pathetic? "Well, it would be awkward if they got the wrong idea. That's all."

A tight, almost sad smile played across his lips. "You don't think our little wager got them talking? Think I didn't get rousted?"

Oddly enough, the thought hadn't crossed her mind. But now that she thought about it, of course they'd be curious. "What did they say?"

Running his hand through his hat-flattened curls, he studied her face as though uncertain.

"Mac, what did they say?"

He shrugged his shoulders. "They're making some wagers of their own, that's all."

Her muscles tensed. *Wagers? Dear Lord, I can only imagine…* She shifted her weight defensively. "What kind of wagers?"

A real smile touched his lips as he took in her stance. "You started this, sweetheart. Don't look at me as though I let some cat out of a bag. I'm the victim here."

"What cat? What bag? What do you mean 'victim?'"

"You set me up, remember—hook, line, and sinker. Now, I'm riding a nasty-mean bull and listening to jokes about marriage and being hen-pecked or some such crap."

She gasped—a genuine inhalation of horror. "They

did not!"

"Of course they did, they're guys."

It was exactly what she'd been trying to avoid. Exactly. The last thing she'd wanted was to be hooked once more to one of the Palmer brothers. It simply made her look…sad, really, really sad.

Laying out her palms in front of her face, she let her head drop. "We have to fix this."

"*We* don't have to do anything," he said, the twang in his Texan deeply pronounced. "This is your doing."

"My doing?" She peeked out from between her fingers then simply let her hands drop. "I'm not the one who made this into a fiasco."

His eyes widened incredulously. "So, my breaking my neck is less of a fiasco than them ribbing me about our love life?"

Her head began to pound. Her shoulders slumped. "We don't have a love life."

"There'd be little point in them placing bets if we did."

He was right, not that it mattered. The real point here was that the damage was done.

"Okay, fine, so we're now running damage control. There's no need to make things worse by you taking the ride. We have to call it off. I'll say I wanted out of the bet. I'll take full responsibility. I don't have a problem with that."

It was his turn to moan. Laying back his head, he rolled it left to right across his shoulders. "Can't," he replied, sounding truly remorseful.

"Don't be ridiculous, of course you can."

"No, I really can't." He looked her way and grinned his all-consuming grin. "Sorry, sweetheart, I have boots that need polishing, a truck that needs cleaned, and a back waiting for the delicate touch of a woman indebted."

She lifted her hands, holding her fingers bent and her nails out as claws. "Ready when you are, dear."

Grabbing her hands, he massaged them flat. "Behave yourself, wildcat, or I'll have you scrubbing the stalls."

"Mighty big talk for someone who has yet to ride the count."

He dropped her hands only to pull her into his arms. He smiled then dropped his lips to hers.

Gone. She was instantly gone, lost in the magic that only a dream come true could let free.

Softly, his lips pressed to hers, caressing, tingling, arousing a desire for more…so much more.

She hung on tight, maybe even desperately, holding her fingers tight in his curls, curls which had tortured her for years, curls which had worked their way into her dreams far more times than she could possibly remember, curls which felt wonderful, *oh yes*, so wonderful.

Her heart pounded, her blood on fire. Her lips were kissing him back and all inhibitions had scattered to gone.

She wanted this, *really* wanted this, really—

What is that? His fingers tapped against her back.

Three. Four. Five.

Wait a second!

She slipped her hands from his hair to grasp on tight to his arms. They were really nice arms— powerful, manly.

Six.

She quit kissing him back and tried to pull away, but he held on tight, holding her against him, feeling better than any man had a right to feel.

Seven.

Dang his hide! She pushed a little harder, but he only tightened his grip and deepened the kiss.

If only it didn't feel so good. If only she weren't so completely turned on.

Eight.

No! No! Not done.

His lips softened then released hers, but his hold around her waist was still firm. He leaned back, his eyes smoldering with more than mere triumph. "If I can handle a wildcat like you for eight seconds, I'm certain I can handle one silly old bull."

He let her go, patting her backside before turning and heading for the kitchen.

Gone.

He was gone, and all she wanted was to have him back.

Chapter Nine

The phone rang and rang.

What was it with her grandparents that they couldn't answer her calls?

Grace looked to the clock on the stove. 10:30 a.m. That made it 8:30 a.m. in Vancouver. Her grandmother should have gotten back from her morning walk with Mrs. Poundstone nearly a half-hour ago.

Typically, right around this time, Myrtle would be sitting at her grandmother's kitchen table, rubbing her calves and running through a list of other neighbors Grandma could be calling for companionship on her "invigorating" walks.

It was a ritual. Myrtle complained while Grandma rummaged around the kitchen, starting the kettle boiling, prepping cups and saucers for tea, and completely ignoring her friend.

On days Grace hadn't had class, she always looked forward to capturing a seat with them. She loved watching the hilarious saga unfold. It was as though neither woman realized its redundancy nor recognized its humor. But Grace had.

The phone rang again. Still no answer.

Odd.

Tapping her fingers against the earpiece, she wondered what had interrupted the friends' routine— something obviously had. Unlike her grandfather, if her grandmother was there, Grace was certain she'd have taken her call.

She placed the phone back on its cradle. If she couldn't check off the day's task one, she'd go after task two—*talk an obstinate cowboy out of doing something stupid.*

She headed down the hall and out onto the veranda. Stopping right before the steps, she took a moment to enjoy the view of a peaceful world in motion. Despite the early hour, Buster's Prairie was already in full swing. The largest hubbub stood, ran, and sauntered around the various pens making up the corral, but a few lent their forms as specks scattered across the mixed canvas.

Far ahead and to her right, Lance headed down the dirt path toward the open range, most likely going after the last few stragglers destined for the chutes. Straight ahead, Mick, dangling a rope over his shoulder, ran from the barn toward the pens. To her left, just outside the fenced-off area that surrounded the chicken coops, Jenny stood holding Ellie. Inside the fence, Tagger tossed feed from a tin bucket onto the ground. Grace laughed along with grandmother and grandchild as the hens, clucking with excitement, swarmed the cowboy's boots, causing him to holler and toss the rest of the feed.

It all made her feel so very alive. Even standing there doing nothing, she felt a part of something glorious. It had always hit her with such force—the sheer magnificence of a life so basic.

Spotting her grandfather and Jarrod standing high on the fences surrounding the round pens, she headed their way. If Mac wasn't with them, he wouldn't be far away.

She'd done a horrible job the night before of getting her point across, so this morning, she was determined. After tossing and turning all night, she knew she couldn't let him ride, not because of her and some silly idea she'd come up with, an idea she never imagined he'd actually take seriously. And it wasn't because she was afraid he'd manage it. It was because she was afraid he wouldn't and be hurt.

Despite years of wishing the man's arrogance would come back to bite him, she didn't want it to be like this, not where more than his pride stood to be injured.

Reaching the fence, Grace climbed up to stand beside Jarrod. Moos and hollers sounded through the yards as the cowboys worked as one to muster the cattle in and through the round pens to the holding area. Dust, along with a not-so-pleasant odor, filled the air.

"Whoa!" Grace wrinkled her nose then waved her hand back and forth in front of it. "It's a little potent here."

The young ranch hand turned her way and grinned. "It's nothing but a bit of nature put back to the ground. Don't tell me you've gone all girlie on me, princess."

Flicking her finger against his shoulder, she tossed him a playful scowl. "Call me princess again, and you're going to be explaining to the men how this *girlie* kicked your ass."

"Ah, just like old times." Her grandfather winked in her direction.

"You and Savannah planning on going to the social this weekend?" she asked Jarrod. "I'm anxious to meet her. Someone's gotta give the girl fair warning."

"Oh, I've warned her plenty about you already." The twinkle in his eyes told her there existed some truth to his words. "She's anxious to meet you as well. And yes, we plan to be there. I got lassoed in by Mac. She got tethered by Tess. There really wasn't a choice."

"For the record, your fearless leader surrendered you all for no more than tea and cookies. It was truly quite shameful. Be sure to tell the others, and feel free to tell Mac I said so."

"We've all been buttered up by Claire's cookies a time or two," Gramps said with a chuckle. "Truth be told, she's had us all by her oven for years."

"So, that's the way to a cowboy's heart, is it?"

"Absolutely." Both men grinned at the other and nodded.

"Pathetic." Grace rolled her eyes, but inside, her heart warmed. She only loved them more for their boyish weaknesses.

Jarrod looked off toward the hills. "Savannah makes a rump roast that can have me salivating before I even reach her front porch."

"It's Patsy's pasta dishes that leave me drooling." Gramps followed his gaze out into the distance and smiled. "But in truth, that woman could make a gourmet meal out of a piece of bologna."

"Grandma's got a knack," she agreed, the very thought of her grandmother's spaghetti making her stomach stir with a craving.

"All this talk about food is making me hungry." Jarrod slapped his hand down against the fence. "Guess I better get busy." He turned to Gramps. "I told Doc I'd help him set up."

In way of permission, her grandfather waved his

hand toward the pen where the vaccines would be given.

Her friend looked back her way. "Want to play some horseshoes a little later?"

"Sure, but I'd rather go to the falls. I thought you were going to play hooky one day and take me?"

Smacking a hand to his forehead, Jarrod moaned. "Not in front of the boss, Grace."

She looked to her grandfather. He smiled.

"Oh, yeah." She pretended to grimace. "Just kidding. Playing hooky would be wrong."

"Great save," Gramps said dryly before looking past her to Jarrod. "I don't care if you take a day to take Grace to the falls, but you'll need to run it by Mac first. Make sure it's good with his schedule."

"The man has a schedule?" From everything she'd seen, he pretty much came and went as he pleased.

"I believe your grandfather is referring to his schedule for his crew, which includes me." Jarrod hopped down from the fence.

Grace scowled. She'd been trying to get to the falls for days now, but one thing after another kept hindering her plans, and usually that something could be trailed back to Mac. She was beginning to believe he didn't want her to go.

"If Grandfather says it's all right, you really shouldn't have to ask any further," she declared. "I say we go tomorrow."

"I'm not going without Mac's okay, Grace." Jarrod turned and headed for the northern pen.

"This isn't a sacred journey," she hollered after him. "You don't need his blessing."

Her old friend simply stuck his hand in the air and

waved.

Her grandfather chuckled behind her.

"What's so funny?"

He merely grinned. "Sometimes, I swear it's like looking in a mirror. How is it your grandmother can find you so lovable, yet find *me* so annoying?" He patted the space on the fence left vacant beside him.

She shuffled down the boards his way. "I don't know what you're talking about. We're both perfectly lovable. Jarrod's just being stubborn, and he's not alone. Every time I ask someone to take me to the falls, they always say they have to check with Mac. And *that* always leads to a *no-can-do*. I don't understand why they even have to ask. This is your ranch, Gramps. If you're okay with it, I fail to see why Mac has to even be involved."

"You've been here long enough. I'm sure you've realized who's actually running the show these days."

"You're still signing their checks."

"Maybe, but he's still their boss. I've told you before. The men respect Mac. They love you, Grace, every one of them, but you needn't test their loyalties. They belong first with him."

"Hmph." The truth of it annoyed her. She scoured the pens. "Speaking of Mac, where is the lord of the rings?"

"Left early this morning for Dallas."

"Dallas? What for?"

"Supplies."

"I thought we had supplies delivered?"

"We do for the most part, but this was a special order."

"Aren't I supposed to know about special orders?"

173

"Let's go help the men move the cattle through the squeezing gate," he said, moving down off the fence and purposefully ignoring the question. "Those cows can be difficult."

"They're not the only things around here with that shortcoming," she muttered, following him down.

The sound of a plane hummed from the distance. Shading their eyes, they both looked to the hills. The first glimpse of a small plane arrived at their peaks. She swallowed, and her stomach turned. It was way too early to be Mac, which most likely meant it was his brother.

Catching her worried expression, her grandfather reached out and squeezed her hand. "It's a moment bound to see its time. May as well see it pass."

He was right, of course. Still, if she'd been given the choice, she undoubtedly would have postponed the moment as long as possible. She felt terribly unprepared and uncomfortably outnumbered—Garrett, now married and bringing his sidekick, counting as two, her still being one.

"Come on, Grace. Let's make ourselves useful." Gramps turned to follow Jarrod's trail to the northern pen.

She seriously thought about taking a quick exit right. One dash, the opening of a door, and a flight of stairs, and she could hide out in her room until their visit was over.

Sayonara. Adios. Arrivederci.

But instead, she followed behind her grandfather, shoulders slumped, feet surly dragging.

Several minutes later, sitting on the fence beside the squeeze chute, awaiting her next call to duty, she watched the old battered work truck make its way down from the airstrip, a cloud of dust leaving a trail in its wake.

There was a time the thought of Garrett coming home had filled her with excitement. Now, outside of the trepidation, she felt surprisingly little. She'd expected more—some remnant of the excitement, a thrill, a spark, but they were gone, and not even pain stepped forward to fill the void.

Doc Hamby slapped the patient in front of him on the rear, sending her forward for Jarrod and Gramps to escort back out to the corral. Looking back up to Grace, he hollered, "Next."

She opened the chute. "The doctor will see you now."

The black and white miss slowly sauntered forward without any form of acknowledgement.

Several patients later, Grace spotted Garrett heading around the barn their way. He'd already seen her, his stride faltering ever so slightly as he hesitated and shortly thereafter waved.

Except for the discomfort of an uncomfortable situation, she still felt surprisingly little. Taking a deep breath, she lifted her hand and waved back.

He hadn't changed all that much, other than his form had matured, broadening and filling out as men tend to do. His hair was cut much shorter, a different look, neither better nor worse.

"Garrett!" A round of greetings followed his arrival to the pen.

He acknowledged them all with jabs and ribs, his glances occasionally drifting her way.

Just like his brother, he completely dashed her

fantasies of finding him beaten and haggard by the years. He was still quite handsome, though for some reason, she found the truth less annoying with him.

It felt odd, sitting back from it all, watching him interact with the others like she had a million times before. It was a bit like watching a show that only halfway held her interest. He was a nice enough guy and always had been. But as hard as she tried, she couldn't remember what she'd found so appealing.

"Next," Doc called, sending her into motion.

"Come on, sexy." She swung the gate open. A pair of wide brown eyes stared forward from a motionless frame.

Standing on the boards behind the squeezing pen, Brody prodded the cow to take action. And so it continued through the next couple hours until he hollered, "That's it, folks."

Grace hopped down from her perch on the fence. "I'll throw some lunch together and have it on the front-porch table in ten." Without looking for any formal acknowledgment, she slipped between the pen's boards and headed for the house.

She'd sensed Garrett was waiting to talk with her, so it came as no surprise when he caught up with her halfway to the house.

"Grace, got a minute?"

She weighed her options—fight or flight. Then, of course, there was always *man-up*, a stupid phrase that had always slightly annoyed her.

Stopping only a couple feet from a clear getaway, she turned. "Sure." She was plenty good with calling it over and pretending nothing had ever happened, but apparently, it wouldn't be that easy.

Fidgeting with the hat he held in his hands, Garrett hesitated a moment before confessing, "It's hard to know where to begin."

Not particularly excited to help him, but still eager to get away, she offered. "It's done and over. You needn't say anything at all."

"I'm sorry, Grace." Bowing his head, he shook it. "Doesn't amount to much, does it?"

"It's fine. Everything turned out for the best." She was skating through on autopilot, simply looking forward to having this conversation behind them, not truly caring how they got there other than fast.

"It was cowardly not to tell you myself, to leave it the way I did."

She nodded. Four years equaled a lot of time brooding over the facts. This one she knew he had right.

"If it helps, I've kicked myself plenty over the years, and not just because of the multiple ear-bashings I've received from…well, many. I simply regret it. I'm ashamed of it. And I've been miserable over the thought of how I hurt you." He raised his head. "My only excuse you might find poor, but the truth is I was weak, dumb, and young. I cared about you, Grace. I still do. That's what always had me so confused. I didn't understand the difference. I loved you, but I wasn't in love with you. I realized it when I met Jackie."

It came as a shock, realizing how much she'd needed to hear it—the apology, the remorse. They, she and him, weren't meant to be together. He didn't have to tell her, she'd already figured it out, but she'd needed the rest—the validation that she'd meant something, that he knew how much he'd hurt her, and that he cared.

The muscles she'd unconsciously held tight slowly began to release as the tension of a moment she'd dreaded for years escaped into history. She managed what she hoped wasn't too awkward a smile. "Thank you."

"Do you think you'll ever be able to forgive me?"

"I think I already have. But I need time to…process everything."

His lips pulled tight as he looked down, emphasizing the moment had been no easier for him.

"I care about you, too, Garrett, and I'm fine. Truly. You did us both a favor that night. It's taken me a while to realize it, but I do."

He nodded, and like her, attempted a smile.

"Ellie's amazing by the way."

His smile relaxed and grew huge. "She is, isn't she? I'm crazy about her, Grace. That little girl has me wrapped a million times around her finger."

She grinned. "Well, you've got a lot of company wrapped right there with you. Your mother is simply in heaven. The kid even has Mac cooing and gushing."

He wrinkled his nose. "It's a hard thing to watch, isn't it? It just doesn't quite fit."

They both laughed. But in truth, she'd secretly loved watching Mac interact with his niece. It was something she was having a very hard time forgetting. He'd been so open, gentle, so completely enchanted—it was a side of the man she'd never before seen, and one she had to admit she wouldn't mind seeing again.

****

"Three out of three." Jarrod rubbed his knuckles against his chest in a boastful manner. "I'd say that makes Grace and me the champs."

Garrett rolled his eyes then pointed to her. "You've got the reigning queen of horseshoes on your team." Nodding to the raven-haired beauty at his side, he added, "I've got a novice. Of course you're going to win."

"Thanks, dear, for the love and support." Jackie's dry monotone spoke volumes of her thoughts.

No matter how hard Grace tried not to like the woman, she did, not that it surprised her all that much. She'd liked her the first time she'd met her, as well. Though in truth, it had only been in passing.

Jackie had come to the ranch with her father to deliver a bull.

The men had all been smitten—Jarrod, Tagger, Brody, and now thinking back, she could recognize the signs of interest in Garrett as well, though at the time she'd denied it to herself. Denial had gotten her through a lot back then—never questioning Garrett's frequent trips away from the ranch, never questioning the distance that had emerged so loudly between them.

Garrett grimaced then grinned at his wife. "Sorry, honey, you simply need a little practice."

"Let's even the odds." Grace made her way to her opponents' side of the pit and placed her arm through Jackie's. "The pro and the novice against the braggart and the whiner."

Garrett scowled. "Did you seriously just call me a whiner?"

"He isn't a particularly good loser." Jackie purposefully added oil to the fire.

"Oh, you are so on." He pointed a finger first to his wife then Grace. "Come on, Jarrod." He stomped his way across the sand to his recently bestowed partner. "Let's teach these ladies a little something about man power."

"Man power?" Jackie cast a humorous look in her direction. "Doesn't that require a remote?"

"And I believe a recliner," Grace added, exchanging a boisterous high-five with her new partner.

"Very funny," Jarrod said.

Garrett rolled his eyes and folded his arms across his chest. "Maybe the two of you being friends isn't such a good idea after all."

"No." The ranch hand eyed the stake in the ground through the center of his raised horseshoe. "The little women merely need put in their place. Come on, Garrett. Let's show them how it's done."

Jackie leaned closer to her and whispered, "They're so easily rattled."

"Watch and learn, ladies." Jarrod took a step forward, letting loose the horseshoe to make a ringer.

Heads swelled and chests inflated right before her eyes. "This should be interesting," she said to Jackie.

And it turned out to be just that. Both men were decent players, and Jackie really did rule the top of the *worst* list. Despite several attempts to give her pointers, her natural lack of talent always shined through.

"Sorry," she offered, standing beside Grace, watching the two men do a pitifully boastful dance.

Grace smiled to reassure her. "It's one and one. We'll take them round three."

The purr of a distant engine rolled their way from behind a beautiful orange sky. They all turned toward the hills, where a couple seconds later, a plane emerged.

Mac had returned.

An odd yet familiar lightness descended around Grace's heart. Her pulse quickened. She found herself delighted, eager, longing to run down the path that would take her directly to the landing strip.

This was the reaction she'd looked for earlier and not found with Garrett. In truth, she couldn't remember ever having it quite like that with him. Its familiarity came from a time even further back, a time when she'd awoken every morning with an uncontrollable zest, eager to find the boy who made every second seem enriched with wonder and possibility. It was the same giddy sense of happiness that she'd felt way back then.

How could she be so foolish? How could her sense and senses betray her so completely? They'd taken the beatings right along with her heart. Could they not remember? Had they no stronger need for self-preservation? Thank goodness her head now ruled them all, because she was certain the man would break her heart again if she dared give him the chance.

Standing beside her, following the plane's approach, Jackie shifted her weight to watch Grace. "When I first came to Buster's Prairie, I thought it was the two of you who were the item."

"Mac and I?" Her voice sounded somewhat animated, like Scooby Doo being asked to follow a gremlin.

Her new friend grinned. "Yes. Is it so unimaginable?"

Grace blinked. "You have no idea. Whatever made you think we were a couple?"

Jackie smiled as she once again scanned the sky. "The way he looked at you."

"With daggers and revulsion?"

"Revulsion?" The raven-haired beauty laughed as she shook her head. "I'm certain what I saw had nothing to do with revulsion. Just like I'm certain that look I saw on your face a moment ago had nothing to do with indifference."

"Are you two going to stand their jabber-jawing, or are we going to finish this?" Jarrod pointed down toward their stake.

"Well, aren't you in a hurry to lose?" Grace brushed off Jackie's ridiculous misconception and turned her attention back to the game. She couldn't listen to such nonsense. She'd lived in a dream world for too many years as it were. Never again would she lead her life by unlikely hopes and wishful maybes.

"Actually…" Garrett handed the horseshoe he held in his hand over to Jarrod. "The game's going to have to wait. I brought the truck down from the airstrip, remember? I'm going to have to go pick up Mac."

The front door's screen crashed against the home's siding.

"Is that the plane I heard?" Her grandfather stood on the veranda shading his eyes as he looked out toward the hills.

Spotting the plane before receiving his answer, he shot down the steps and raced as fast as she'd seen him move in years across the gravel drive to the truck. The door flew open, her grandfather crawled in, and in near the next second, the engine turned and the truck went flying.

The old lion appeared to have swallowed some hefty catnip.

"Hmm." Garrett watched with the rest of them as a ball of dust circled behind the truck, blocking it and the road ahead from their view. "Guess the game doesn't have to wait after all."

****

Mac spotted the second plane off to the side of the runway the moment they passed the ridge.

So, it was already done. By now, Grace and Garrett had probably already spoken. He couldn't even imagine how it had gone down. She seemed all right. Most of her anger seemed to have dissipated, and most of what had been there had been more directed at him than his brother anyway.

Still, he was curious.

"Ooh." At his side, his passenger sighed and crossed her arms over her chest. It was as though she were trying to capture and hold in the emotions suddenly overtaking her. Tears welled in her eyes as she glanced his way. "I'd forgotten how beautiful it all is. How could I have forgotten? How could I have stayed away so long?"

Affection rose as warmth in his heart. He'd missed her. "I'm just glad you're back. Welcome home, Patsy."

Her face lit to radiant. "Thank you, Mac. It's really good to be here." Lifting her hands to cover her mouth, she breathed in deep, closed her eyes, and took a minute to steady herself. When she opened her eyes, they were filled with worry. "I really hope I'm doing the right thing. It's been hard starting over. I wouldn't want to have to do it again, especially alone."

Now that he understood her reason for staying gone so long, he was confident in his answer. "You belong here, Patsy. Eldon knows that as well as you."

She'd simply been waiting for her husband to ask, a fact she'd made Mac promise he'd never reveal. But heaven help him, if the old codger didn't get with the game and tell her his true feelings, Mac knew he'd have a hard time not kicking his dear old friend's backside with a few matters of fact.

"Grace is going to be so excited." Patsy smiled at the thought. "She wanted me to come with her. I probably should have, though I can't say I'm sorry for waiting." She laughed and looked his way. "Silly, aren't I, needing to hear he needed me?"

Still watching the sky, Mac did his best to reassure her. "I don't believe it's so strange. We all need to feel needed."

He heard her shift in her seat to face him directly. "So, how is she?"

"She seems to be settling in all right."

"Good, I'm glad to hear it. She loves this place. Although, for a while, I think she forgot that." His dear friend took a deep breath and leaned back in her seat. "I wouldn't want what happened between her and Garrett to forever cloud her view of the ranch. It's the only home she's ever really known. I believe it's important the memories remain good ones."

He couldn't agree more. Hopefully, the next two years would allow him a chance to help her build memories much happier than in years past.

"There it is." He pointed to the make-shift landing strip. "The landing's not the smoothest you'll find. So you might want to hold on."

"I'll be all right." Her smile was back. She was way too eager to be scared.

Mac spotted his touch-down point and dumped the plane's flaps, causing it to drop. The tires hit the hard earth and gravel, spitting back rock as they settled onto the path.

Patsy held tight to her seat as they rolled to a stop. When the plane had sat idle a moment, she turned his way. "Well, that will take some getting used to."

He grinned. "The gravel limits my choices, not one of them smooth. I prefer the spot, drop, and roll method as it gives me better visibility and keeps the plane and its tail from getting too badly beaten."

"Ever consider asphalt?"

"It's coming, but not until fall. There aren't a lot of asphalt companies out this direction. We're on a list, waiting our turn."

"Ah," she said, nodding, "now I remember a drawback. Nothing ever happens quickly in the remote Texas hills."

He laughed. "Many see that as a perk. I take it you don't?"

"Let's just say I see its downside as well." She unbuckled the belt strapping her in.

"I'll come around and help you down." After releasing his constraints, he pushed open the door. Not far down the dirt path, he could see their taxi making haste their way. He was less than surprised to later see Eldon sitting behind the wheel. When the man wanted to, he could seriously move.

Mac helped Patsy down then pointed her toward the truck now rolling to stop beside the other plane. "I'll be a minute getting your bags. Why don't you run ahead and say your hellos?"

Watching her make her way to the battered vehicle and the old man now stepping out onto the gravel, Mac said a silent prayer the old fool could handle the amazing opportunity he was being given without placing his foot too deeply into his mouth.

Rounding the plane, he kept himself busy with one unnecessary chore after the other, providing them time he hoped they both would use wisely. By the wide smiles on their faces as he headed their way, he assumed they'd managed it well.

"Ready?" Mac lowered the suitcases into the truck's bed. He'd been thrilled to notice earlier, by the weight of her luggage and their size, she was likely planning a lengthy stay.

"We're ready." Eldon pulled up just right on the old truck's handle, opening it with an ease reflecting years of practice. He stepped back and tenderly took Patsy's hand. With the care a man would give a precious heirloom, he guided her into the cab.

Mac's heart gave a little tug. That was the beauty of sharing your life with another, to have someone you knew, someone who knew you so well, that you both understood the true value of the other. His thoughts drifted further to a particularly spunky brunette. No one would deny her beauty, but how many would understand her full worth?

The horn blew. Eldon was turned in his seat looking back at him. "We heading home today, Sleeping Beauty, or are you waiting for your prince?"

Yep, a true treasure. Mac smiled, shook his head, and moved to the cab's driver's side.

A few short minutes later, he pulled the old truck into the yard. To say the least, he was surprised by the foursome he spotted playing horseshoes in the yard as though they'd all been friends forever. His attention, of course, focused immediately on Grace.

She glanced their way, squinted, took a couple

steps closer, and squinted again. The horseshoe fell from her fingers as a breathtaking smile spread across her face. Covering her mouth with her hands, she squealed and did a funny kind of dance before sprinting their way.

His heart tightened and beat a little faster. Without any doubt, he was simply crazy for the woman. He sighed, wishing it could be him she was so excited to see. But that was an opportunity he himself had let slip by. Now, she didn't even know he was there, so he'd simply watch, enjoying the moment for what it was.

Eldon slid out of the truck then turned to help Patsy down.

"Grandma!" Grace flew at the older woman like a linebacker aiming for a sack. Throwing her arms around her, she squeezed tight. "I can't believe you're here."

Patsy laughed then kissed her granddaughter's cheeks before stepping back. "Me neither, but I'm sure glad I am. Your grandfather asked me to come. He thought you might be lonely without me. But from the looks of things, you're doing quite nicely."

"Yes, but never better than now." Grace reached out to pull both her grandparents into a happy circle.

Mac smiled, happy for the family that was, but yet wasn't, his.

Grace caught his expression over her grandparents' shoulders. She smiled back then mouthed the words, *Thank you.*

Simple and not surprising, yet filling him with delight, her gratitude brought him hope—hope that one day it would be his arms that held her, and his return that brought her such joy.

****

Closing her eyes and lifting her feet, Grace leaned back in the tree swing and let the forces of nature do the rest. Around and around she went, the wind whipping through her hair, pulling forth a rush of nostalgia that quickly overtook the moment.

She'd spent hours on the wood swing as a child, never dreaming of being any place other than right there on the ranch or perhaps flying in the air above. It was her heaven on earth, and everything she thought she'd ever need…well, almost everything.

The cords broke free only to spin together again for a couple wounds in the other direction, stopping with a slight jolt to fall back to a halt. The world spun softly in her head as a shadow stepped in front of her unseen light. Opening her eyes, she looked directly into Mac's.

He tilted back his hat. "Having fun?"

"As a matter of fact," she said with a grin, "I am."

Strolling leisurely behind her, he gave her a gentle push. "How's Patsy settling in?"

The breeze felt nice against her skin. Lifting her legs, she began to pump. "Wonderfully, I believe. She seems really happy to be back."

He pushed again. "I think she is. It was sure great to see her."

Closing her eyes once more, Grace smiled, lifting her face up to the sun. The swing reached its peak then swung back down. She waited anxiously for the feel of Mac's hands against her back.

They were there, strong but gentle, sending her farther back into the sky where the sun's warmth reached down to kiss her forehead before gravity pulled her back toward the grass for the thrill of his touch. On one hand, she truly wished he didn't affect her so, but on the other hand, it allowed for so much—the utter excitement arising from something as simple as a touch, the thrill of senses heightened with anticipation.

At that moment, she felt on top of the world. How many times had she dreamt of such a moment as a child—as a young woman? Countless. For years, she'd waited out on the yard for his return from the range, only to have him skirt her completely on his way back to his home.

The memory stole a bit of her joy. Letting her legs drop, she allowed her feet to drag across the ground. She eventually stopped right in front of him.

"Had enough?" he asked from behind.

Leaning her head against the rope, she sighed. "Yeah."

He walked out in front of her and took a seat on the grass. "You seem troubled. Is everything all right?"

Never one to let a perfect opportunity slip her by, she smiled. "I'm having a little problem with a rather stubborn cowboy."

Stretching out his long legs, he leaned back on his elbows and smiled. "You don't say? Anyone I know?"

"Know many cowboys too stubborn to listen to reason?"

He laughed, nodding toward the sky. "I know a few."

Rubbing her hands across her face, she groaned with exasperation. "Will it do me any good to ask again?"

He grinned, shook his head. "Not an ounce."

"Stubborn fool."

He laughed again. "Probably."

Grace enjoyed the sound of his laugh—deep, solid, real. It had a strange way of making her believe all was well in the world. A ridiculous belief considering he was about to place himself on a near two-thousand-pound bull.

She could feel his eyes upon her as his laugh faded to gone. Twirling the swing very lightly, she lifted and lowered her feet, allowing the flattened blades of grass beneath to caress their tips. "How long have you known my grandmother was coming?"

"A couple weeks, but until late last night, not even Eldon knew when for sure. I'm surprised he kept it a secret from you so long. He's been like a youngster waiting on Christmas—very eager, annoyingly impatient."

"Sounds like my grandfather." She looked his way. "They both seem really happy. I think they'll work things out."

"I hope so." Picking a particularly long piece of grass, he threw it into the air and watched it twirl its way back down to the ground. "Things went all right with Garrett?"

"Yeah, fine. Everything's…" For the first time, it struck her how truly amazing it was. She paused and embraced the truth of it.

"Grace?"

She smiled. "Everything's really good actually."

Lifting a curious brow, he searched her face as though looking for confirmation. "It couldn't have been easy."

"No, but I wouldn't say it was hard either. We've both changed."

"Grown up." He held her gaze as he picked another

piece of grass and then another. "It happens to everyone. Well, most everyone anyway."

"Yes," she said, fighting a smile, "and I'm sure one day it will happen for you as well."

He grinned and tossed his fistful of grass her way. "Simply can't help yourself, can you?"

"Not easily. You know what they say—old habits die hard." She smiled unrepentantly. "Especially ones you rather enjoy."

Moving forward onto one knee, he pushed himself to standing. Then, much to her surprise, he lifted her out of the swing to toss her over his shoulder. Holding on tight, he swung her around and around.

"Mac!" His name flew into the air with giggles and screams. She pounded against his back until he finally stopped and they both dropped to the ground.

The world spun as they lay on their backs and laughed up at the sky.

"That was stupid." He turned his head her way. "Now, I think I'm sick."

"Wait until Last Ride sets you twirling."

He rolled to face her. "I'm going to make the count. You're going to be mine."

"Yeah, yeah, I know. Then I'll be polishing boots and spit-shining stirrups." She rolled to face him. "I've heard the stories. I'm still not scared. There's a lot of distance between talking the talk and riding the ride."

Mac's gaze drifted past her to the arena. "That there is."

"Sure you don't want to postpone the ride until after the dance? It might be a bit embarrassing toting a shiner around on the dance floor."

"The only thing shining will be my boots." He

tossed her a crooked smile. "Or at least they will be if you do your job right."

"Save your hype, cowboy, and get my passport ready."

"You're merely digging yourself a longer chore list, pretty lady." He moved to his feet then offered her his hand.

She placed hers in his, and he pulled her up. For a moment, she stood still in front of him, enjoying the feel of his touch, the thrill of having him near. They'd come a long way over the last few weeks.

I'd be a fool to see too much into it.

She pulled back her hands and got back to the point. "Mac, all kidding aside, I do wish you'd reconsider."

Reaching out, he pulled a piece of grass off the side of her cheek. "I'm going to be all right, Grace. But thanks for caring." He leaned forward and kissed the cheek where the grass had lain. Then he turned away and headed toward his mom's place.

Her heart felt as though it could dance on air as she cupped the cheek with her hand and embraced the warmth that lingered. How could something so simple feel so amazing?

She sighed.

What am I doing? It was just a friendly kiss.

Dropping her hand back down to her side, she watched him until he completely disappeared.

Her heart instantly sank.

Oh no!

Chapter Ten

Garrett appeared outside the bucking chute where Mac waited. "Where there's a bad idea, there's a cowboy," he said. Then scratching his head, he asked, "Or is it, where there's a cowboy, there's a bad idea?"

"Never heard either." Mac pushed his hand inside his riding glove then flexed his fingers and palm. Looking over the gate's boards to his brother, he grinned. "I think you're making it up."

"How about, 'pride cometh before the fall?'" His mother stepped up behind Garrett, looking no happier than she had the night before when she'd delivered a ten minute long lecture on the cost of stupidity.

Mac grinned. "Sounds like a loser's cheer to me."

"Best not be mocking the Lord's words right at this moment, young man."

"No worries, Mom. It's your words I'm mocking."

She wrapped her arms around Garrett. "You always were my favorite son."

Mac exchanged a knowing glance with his brother. They'd both been tossed that role, depending on who'd been naughty and who'd been nice, since they were teenage boys. Truth be told, Jenny Palmer-Hamby couldn't have loved either one of them any more than she did.

His mother reached over the chute to take his hand. "You be careful, Mac. Don't give that bull a chance to hurt my son."

"Don't worry." He winked. "I've got this."

She sighed, shaking her head. "Where have I heard that before?" Then, not waiting for an answer, she walked away.

Garrett's gaze met his. "You're right, you know. You can do this." He slapped the gate, turned, and followed his mother across the arena toward the small gathering.

Mac appreciated their support, he always did. But in truth, he knew he had this one. It was an odd kind of certainty he'd held all along, one which had evaded him on rides prior.

"Ready, Mac?" Brody hollered from the holding pen.

He shifted to look behind him then waved his hand high in the air. "Bring him down."

"Last chance, cowboy." Grace suddenly appeared outside his chute.

With her Stetson sitting tilted at the perfect angle, her blue eyes sparkling, and her long hair picking up the sun's rays to shine like gold, she made the sexiest picture he ever had seen.

She grinned. "You don't have to do this, you know. No one will think less of you if you cower and run."

Heaven help him, she had more sass than the bull who'd soon be heading down the passage.

He leaned forward over the boards. "Keep it up, sweetheart. I'm thinking up all sorts of fun little projects for you."

She shrugged her shoulders. "I'm not scared." Nodding her head back toward the holding pen, she added, "I've been over there taunting Last Ride, giving him a little encouragement to…you know, keep the ride interesting."

He wouldn't put it past her to badger the bull. There was definitely no doubt she was prodding the rider. He could hardly wait to get off the beast just to get to her. The woman was absolutely irresistible when she was misbehaving.

Reaching out over the boards, he flicked the tip of her hat. "Go take your seat, Grace. I don't need more than one force of ornery inside that ring."

Batting her lids, she raised her hand to her chest and in the sweetest southern drawl he'd ever heard, declared, "I'm certain I have no idea what it is you're talking about." Her nose went high in the air. Pointing across the arena to where a full audience already stood waiting, she dropped the accent and added, "I'll take my sunshine over there." She looked back over her shoulder, gracing him with a smile. "If you miss me, I'll be the one with the pompoms rooting for the bull."

"You wait, sunshine," he yelled as he watched her magnificent swing carry her back across the dirt. "Your time's coming, and sweetheart, I'll show you no mercy."

Her swing never missed a beat, taunting him with an indifference he wanted badly to address. Sliding between the boards of the fence, she disappeared behind the other spectators only a moment before nudging herself a spot beside them.

If her intent had been to distract him, she'd succeeded beautifully. Covering his face with his hands, he rubbed vigorously as he forced himself to refocus.

The banging of boards accompanied the heated

snorts of the roused bull coming down the shafts behind him.

Jarrod jumped up on the opposite side of the bucking chute. "He likes his rights and knows how to deliver them. I'd love to tell you where he goes from there, but he changes it all the time. I never could predict him, so I simply watched my seat. Here he comes," he added, stepping to the back of the small pen, waiting to close the back gate as Last Ride stepped in.

A mass of brown and white bulk stepped forward into the pen. Metal slapped against metal, locking the beast in place. Last Ride lifted his head and snorted his contempt, his huge form vibrating as though flexing for battle.

"You're in for a ride." Brody stood outside the boards at Mac's right, holding the belled-rope. "That bull's ready to rumble." He handed the opposite side of the belt to Jarrod then grabbed the hook lying against the boards. Ducking low, he reached through the chute and grabbed the opposite end of the rope his buddy now had hanging low under the bull. Hooking it, he pulled it under Last Ride then handed it up.

Mac grabbed the rope, straddled the chute, then pulled the cord through its loop and secured it.

"Got it?" Brody asked.

"It's good." He made sure Last Ride knew he was coming before placing himself down on his unappreciative host.

The bull's muscular mass rippled like an over-stimulated, steroid-enhanced six-pack readying to lift and throw a heavily stacked barbell.

Brody was right. He was in for a ride.

Jarrod reached into his pocket and pulled out a can of rosin. Removing the lid, he held it out to Mac.

"Thanks." He took a dab and rubbed it into his glove. The sticky substance would help secure his hold, and by the looks of things, he'd need all the help he could muster. Wrapping the remains of the braided rope around his gloved hand, he cinched it tight, testing it more than once to make sure the hold was secure.

"Good?" Brody asked.

He nodded. "Good."

Both ranch hands shifted their positions along the metal portion of the pen, readying themselves for the ride and all that might come.

Mac adjusted his protective vest then tested once more his grip before raising his free hand into the air and taking a deep breath.

A late bout of nerves trickled in from out of nowhere. He shook them off.

This is it. Ready or not, I've come too far to back out now.

After saying a silent prayer, he gave a quick nod. The gate flew open, and he and the beast below him jolted out into the arena.

Mac's body lurched forward as Last Ride's front legs hit the ground seconds before his thunderous thighs landed behind him. Like a powerful rocket, they immediately exploded into the air, not leaving Mac much time to pull in a breath before his body was jolted again, this time harder, leaving a good cushion of distance between backside and beast.

It was the move to the right Jarrod had mentioned, and like his buddy, Mac was left no option but to watch his seat, pull in his thighs and will his backside to land back on the bull.

It did, but he wasn't given much taste of the victory before he was catapulted back into the air. A twist to the left, a kick to the right, a hurricane and tilt-to-his-world later, and the surrounding audience broke out into cheers, their shouts of jubilee telling him more than the bell that he'd taken the ride clear to the final count.

With great appreciation, he accepted the bull's final buck as his opportunity to dismount. He dropped the rope and swung his leg, landing with a nasty plunk directly on his back. Last Ride twisted again, landing directly in front of him. Eighteen-hundred pounds of unhappy bull stared him down.

The crowd gasped.

Jarrod and Brody were instantly in the ring, running toward the bull.

The beast snorted a heated breath, dripping moisture from his snout as he dug his hoof into the ground.

Mac eyed the bull's horns, for the first time honestly imagining how they'd feel lodged between his ribs.

A hard slap sounded from behind the snarling monster. The bull snapped his head around toward his rear then moved his mass toward Lance, his antagonizer, as Mick and Tagger entered the arena from behind Mac and helped him to his feet.

Lance took off on a run, and Mac and his helpers made a beeline for the fence. The next time he turned around, the arena was clear and Last Ride's large hind end was sauntering lazily down the western chute.

That was a little too close for comfort. He took a slow, calming breath, letting his joints, as well as his emotions, fall back into place.

He owed his men a boot-load of thanks.

"That was one hell of a ride, son," Eldon said, coming up beside him, looking a bit white as he slapped Mac's back.

"Good job" and "congratulations" soon flew from every direction, but there was no sign of the sassy miss who'd so boisterously taunted him from outside his chute. He found her soon enough once the others started to clear. Standing beside his mother where they'd stood all along, both women wore wary expressions that could easily have been mirrored.

The last few seconds of his bout in the ring had apparently had a greater effect on them than the first eight.

His mother was the first to move. Peeling away her hands from the death-grip she'd had on the fence, she wiped them across her jeans then met him halfway. "Well," she said, releasing a heavy sigh, "I sure hope you have that one out of your system."

He smiled, accepting his hat from Phil, who'd gone in and pulled it out of the arena's center. "Never again." And at that moment, he really meant it. The look in Last Ride's eyes had assured him he was only running on God's good graces.

"You're a smart man, my son." She grinned and gave a nod over her shoulder. "Better go collect your prize."

"Believe me. I intend to." Dusting off his hat, he snuck a glance in Grace's direction.

She was shaking. Those lovely blue eyes, which had sparkled with sheer deviltry, now glistened behind unshed tears.

Placing his hat on the post beside him, he brushed the dirt out of his hair as he headed her way.

She swallowed then cleared her throat as she stepped away from the fence to face him. "Nice ride."

Stopping in front of her, he tilted his head and studied her pale complexion. "Were you worried?"

"No." She shook her head, and a tear slipped from the corner of her eye to run down her cheek.

Lifting his hand, he wiped it away. "No?"

The shake slowly turned into a nod as she looked down to the dirt beneath them.

"The men had my back. I was never in danger."

Beautiful blue eyes, surrounded by long, damp lashes glanced up. "I should never have suggested it. I should never have baited you. Mac, I'm sorry."

"It was the best ride of my life and bound one day to happen. I'm not easily baited into anything, Grace. You know that about me. When has it ever worked for you before?"

She laughed a nervous laugh as she wiped the moisture from her eyes. "It was a really sweet ride."

"And a really sweet win. You, sweetheart," he said, trailing his dusty finger down her adorable nose, "are officially mine."

****

Standing at the bottom of the hallway stairs, Grace stared at the handsome cowboy in utter disbelief. "To the falls?" she repeated. "Seriously?"

By all appearance pleased with her reaction, Mac grinned. "Seriously. Do you have a problem with it?"

"No, I…" Her stomach knotted with an odd mix of excitement and apprehension. She couldn't believe it. What was he up to? He had her over the metaphorical barrel, why would he do something nice? There had to be more to it.

"Why?"

"Why?" His brow lifted high. "I thought you wanted to go?"

"Yes, but—"

Mac leaned in closer, bending his head to where his nose nearly touched hers. "Then why ask why?"

Her heart raced and a warm tingle rushed through her. She found herself at a loss for words.

"Better run upstairs and grab a swimsuit, sweetheart, unless you prefer to *skinny* it?"

She tried not to smile, determined not to reward his bad behavior. "I'll be right back." Accepting the reprieve for what it was, she turned and scrambled up the stairs, trying not to seem too ridiculously happy.

"Don't forget your camera," Mac reminded her from below.

"Right. Thanks." She hurried around the corner then ran to her room. "All right, Grace, don't start seeing too much into this," she cautioned herself as she searched her top drawer for her yellow two-piece. Ever since the kiss, she'd been having a hard time reining in her fantasies—fantasies she'd worked very hard to get rid of for years.

She found the swimsuit and pulled it out. Modest as far as bikinis went, but still sexy in a classical way. She'd fallen in love with it twice—once on the manikin where it had promised her perfection and then again when she tried it on. It hadn't delivered perfection, but it came close enough, hiding the slight bulge that had been refusing to leave her middle since as long back as she could remember.

She quickly changed, wearing the bikini beneath her favorite jeans and a simple white T-shirt. With the camera in its case and dangling from her wrist, she stopped by the dresser's mirror on her way out. Not bad, but she could make it better.

"You look lovely." Her grandmother stood in the doorway a moment later, watching her smooth out her hair.

"He's taking me to the falls." Grace shot her a nervous glance before placing the brush down on the dresser. "What do you think he's up to?"

With a soft laugh, Patsy walked into the room. "You can't figure that out?"

"No, I really have no idea. He's been laying down all sorts of threats, and now he says the falls. It makes no sense at all."

Her grandmother appeared in the mirror standing behind her. Lifting her hands, she set them comfortingly on Grace's shoulders. "It makes perfect sense."

She stared back at her through the mirror. "Care to explain?"

Grams smiled and patted her shoulders. "I believe it will be much more fun watching you figure it out on your own."

"Don't go seeing romance in this, Grandma. Believe me, there will be neither roses nor champagne. Mark my words. He's up to something."

"Oh, I believe that." The smile transformed many of the lines she carried on her face into a picture of ageless beauty.

Grace turned to face her, glad she was there. The few weeks they'd been apart had seemed like months.

"I'm glad you've come home, Grandma. What really changed your mind?"

"He told me you needed me."

"Needed you?"

Her grandmother walked away toward the bed. "Yes, I know it's ridiculous. You're a strong woman. I knew you could handle it. If I'd doubted it, I would never have let you come in the first place."

She bit into her lip but couldn't stop the grin.

"Out with it," her grandmother prompted.

"You knew he was baiting you, and you came anyway."

"Your point being?"

"You're still in love with Grandpa."

"Of course I am, and he's still in love with me, though he's having a hard time coming straight out and saying so. Our love isn't a new thing, but as our history has proven, that doesn't mean it's enough. Sometimes what we want isn't what we need."

"Amen to that." She had only minutes ago reminded herself of the very same thing.

Sitting down on the bed, her grandmother traced the quilted pattern of its blue and yellow floral cover. "We have some stark differences, your grandfather and I. I need more than the ranch. He could stay out here forever and never leave. If we're going to work this out, we have to find a compromise. I'm not so certain he's any more willing to budge today than he was four years ago."

"I thought you loved the ranch, Grandma." Grace moved to the bed and sat by her side. "I always got the impression you missed it."

"I have missed it. I love the ranch. I love the

people. But even more than that, I love your grandfather. I love that he has his dream. It's a dream I surrendered an awful lot for and shared with him for many years. But I want to travel. I want to see my son more often. I want Eldon to care enough about me that he'll sacrifice a little of his dream to give me a little of mine."

Leaning forward, she kissed her weathered cheek. "I'm sorry, Grandma. I haven't been the greatest support these last four years. I should have realized you were hurting. I said a lot of things and gave a lot of advice that was really more about me and my circumstance than yours. I'm sure I only made matters worse."

"Oh, honey, I knew the words came from a broken heart. I read you and your truly pathetic advice like a large print novel. You're no more the reason I stayed away than you're the reason I've come back."

"He's been miserable without you. I realized it right away."

Her grandmother smiled. "How is it a girl with such clear vision can be so terribly farsighted when it comes to herself?"

"What do you mean?"

Laughing, Grams reached out and squeezed her hand. "Oh, Gracie, you'll never know how much I love you." Then patting the same hand, she stood. "You go have yourself a good time, young lady. I'm going to stay up here and keep looking for my passport." Shaking her head, she glanced out toward the hallway. "It's the darndest thing. I'd have sworn I left it on my dresser."

No. He didn't!

Grace had to stop herself from laughing out loud. She knew exactly where her grandmother's passport could be found. Much to her delight, it appeared an old dog had learned a new trick.

"Grace." Her grandmother studied her curiously. "Is something wrong?"

"No." She stood and gave her grandma a hug. "I believe everything is just right."

****

Sure, they could have taken separate quads, but where would the fun be in that?

With Grace's arms wrapped tight around him and her body solid against his back, Mac wasn't at all sorry he'd insisted they share the bike...not that she'd at any point argued. Grace Wade may not know it, but she was already on her way to falling in love with him. He didn't care if it took her a million baby-steps to get there, he'd walk with her the entire way, doing whatever he had to do to make sure she got there.

And she would get there.

Luckily, he knew the only insurmountable hurdle wasn't a hurdle for them at all. Attraction not only existed between them, it thrived.

Though he craved the passion, this trip was about something else. They needed to work on other areas— areas that not only needed attention but needed mending as well.

Trust was one such area. She needed to be able to trust him, to know he wouldn't let her down, to know the man he'd become had said goodbye to the selfish boy who had cared little for her feelings.

Today was important.

He wanted the chance to build for her new

memories, better memories, memories where he didn't emerge such a putz. They needed a history that started with them, and he was eager to get it started.

Grace leaned in closer, pressing her cheek against his back. It felt even better than the wind and the thrill of the ride. Having her with him was nothing short of amazing. He pushed down harder on the throttle and held on tight as the bike picked up speed, blasting across the dry bush-covered plains toward the hills.

It took them an hour plus to get to the falls, but the look on her face once they got there made it well worth the time.

"It's so beautiful," she said, looking toward the west where layer upon layer of huge, flat rock created one spectacular waterfall. Lifting her camera, she took one shot after another. "This is proof God's work can't be beat." She moved up a few boulders to get a different angle.

After taking several shots, she turned the lens on him.

He lifted his hand, shooing off the attention. "All right, sweetheart, enough of that."

Still holding the camera in his direction, she moved her head to its side and smiled. "Oh, come on. Don't be shy."

"I'm not shy. I just don't like my picture taken." And that was the truth. It was the residual effect of having to hold still and smile too many times as a child.

Rolling her eyes, she moved back behind the lens and took another shot.

Two quick steps and he'd confiscated the camera.

"Really?" She held out her hand for him to hand the device back. "You have a serious problem with taking things that don't belong to you."

"I'm helping out." He lifted the camera and reversed their roles.

She struck a sexy pose then stuck out her tongue.

"Behave," he warned, finding her adorable all the same and snapping the shot.

She moved up a couple boulders then stopped to shake her head, letting her hair fall all around her in a wild fashion. Then she opened her lips ever so slightly and stared back into the camera. She was being ironic, but it came off sexy all the same.

"Perfect," he said and took the shot.

"See how easy it is?" She jumped down from her perch.

"Of course it's easy for you. You're too cute to take a bad picture."

"Right," she said sarcastically, "like your mug would break a lens."

She reached for the camera, but he caught her around the waist with his free hand and pulled her against him. "You think I'm sexy?"

"I didn't say that."

Still holding her tight, he pursed his lips, giving it serious thought. "Yeah." He wrinkled his nose. "You kind of did."

Biting into her lip, she fought a smile. "You're all right, I guess. Sexy might be stretching it."

"Is that so?" He tickled her side, and she squirmed up against him. "Say, *cheese*." Lowering the camera, he captured them both inside a photo.

"Here, let me see." She reached for the camera. "I wasn't ready. I probably look like a dork."

Mac grinned as he handed it back to her, then

watched over her shoulder as she pulled the picture from memory. A great shot. Not surprisingly, she looked beautiful.

She studied the photo. "I guess you are sort of sexy."

He pointed to the screen. "Certainly you can give me better than 'sort of.'"

Tilting her head, she looked him over. "I'll hold my opinion. I haven't seen you in your trunks yet." She tilted her head to the other side. "Or do you wear Speedos?"

"Speedos! Honestly, Grace, do you know me at all? Besides, I thought you said you wanted to try skinny dipping?"

"You wish."

"As a matter of fact… Are you game? I'll even do a striptease for you." He pulled off his T-shirt then tossed it like a wad of paper. It fell on the long, flat rocks that lined the stream beneath the waterfall.

Sitting down on one of the taller boulders, Grace crossed her legs and grinned. "Really? That's what you call a striptease?"

Not sure what she was after, he flexed his muscles.

She threw back her head and laughed. "Slam-dunking your shirt into the boulders and flexing your pecs does not a striptease make."

"Are you sure?"

"I'm sure. A striptease takes music and moves."

He did a funny dance. "I've got moves."

Grace covered her eyes and moaned. Mac, it turned out, was a terrible dancer. But, man, was he ever fun to watch. By the time he got down to his trunks and bolted for the water, she had nearly laughed herself to tears.

This was a new side to the man, and one she thoroughly enjoyed.

Truth be told, she'd been enjoying his company a lot as of late. Things between them had drastically changed. Her excitement to see him was becoming about more than the attraction. And she was now confident he felt the same.

But what it was, she couldn't yet define, even less, give it a name. All she knew was that for today, for this one, wonderful, magical day, she was going to embrace their time together and pretend like it would never end. What harm could it do as long as they crossed no boundaries?

His water-darkened head bobbed a few feet from the edge. If she hurried, she could douse him before he had time to prepare.

She undressed down to her bikini and then took off on a run. Reaching the water's edge, she jumped boldly off the rock and into the air. Grabbing her legs in her arms, she screamed, "Cannonball!"

Perfect—her aim was perfect, and so was the water, neither warm nor cold. It opened its arms and welcomed her in, cushioning her fall all the way to the bottom. Her feet touched rock, and she jetted back up, breaking through the water only to be caught by a strong pair of arms.

"You tried to drown me," Mac accused, though he sounded anything but concerned.

As the water rolled from the top of her head down over her eyes, she tried to break her arms free from in front of his chest.

Still holding her tight, Mac treaded water. "How do you plead, vixen, guilty or deranged?"

"Innocent!" she declared with impressive conviction, but sadly she was unable to control her funny-bone smile.

He twirled them around in the water to where the sun's light fell directly against her face. "That's hardly the face of an innocent woman."

"Oh, come on, Palmer, even an innocent woman can have a sense of humor, and the look on your face was absolutely priceless."

Pounding his free fist into the water and creating an impressive splash, he moved her directly under its fallout.

She buried her face against his chest, more for the thrill than for the protection.

"So, you admit it. Guilty as charged." He pounded his fist against the water once more.

This time, she closed her eyes and lifted her face as the water sprayed down. Then she opened her eyes and smiled unrepentantly. "You accused me of trying to drown you. That was never my intent."

His hand cupped her face as he spun her again. "You only wanted to scare me?"

The stupid grin wouldn't leave her lips. "I did. I truly did."

"Very well." His voice rose high as he prepared to give judgement. "I find you shameless and sentence you to no less than five dunkings." And with that, he plunged them under.

She wasn't afraid, not for a minute. Instead, she cherished the moments held tight in his arms. Within seconds they were back to the surface, him treading water, keeping them both afloat as she giggled like a school girl being tickled under the monkey bars.

"You hardly seem repentant," he noted.

"I'm not." She laughed, rubbing it in.

His gaze fell to her lips. "I have a better plan."

Before she realized what he was intending, he planted a kiss on her still grinning lips. Together and united, they sank back under. It was surprising and delightful. She'd been waiting days for another kiss, and now that it was here, she wasn't particularly eager to see it end. And neither, it appeared, was he. They sank clear to the bottom, their feet touching the rocks. Then in the form of a moonwalk, they bounced their way across the stones' smooth surfaces.

Her arms broke free only to circle his neck, holding his kiss firm against her lips. Oxygen was an afterthought, and it came a little late. She made for the surface, him coming up directly behind her, pushing her faster.

They emerged one directly after the other, both sputtering water then gasping for air. Grabbing hold of her waist, he swam them to the surrounding rocks. "Are you all right?" His eyes were full of concern.

She coughed, laughed, and then coughed again. "Who's trying to drown whom?"

He grinned a roughish grin that nearly took the breath directly back out of her lungs. "I'm going to call it *time served.*" He moved her against the rocks.

But with her jailer being so fiercely handsome, she didn't want her punishment to end. The moment he backed away, she flicked the water between them up into his face.

He dropped his mouth in an exaggerated look of disbelief. "Really?"

Pushing her feet against the stones behind her, she

launched herself forward into his arms. It was crazy and impetuous and completely contradictory to her usual behavior, but it got her exactly where she wanted to be.

Fortunately, he seemed pleased, wrapping his arms around her and pushing them back into the water where they floated around the pool, enjoying the cool as well as each other.

They stayed for quite some time, chatting about the ridiculous, finding humor in everything—her often clumsy nature, his lack of rhythm, the distant mountain peak that looked a little like Frankenstein. Then they explored the pool's mysteries, of which they found many as they collected souvenirs.

The perfect day.

"Thank you," she said, before kissing him quickly and heading back toward the water's edge.

He swam up beside her. "For what?"

She reached the rocks, and he helped her up to sit on the pool's edge. Once there, she offered him her hand and helped him out to sit beside her.

"For today." She tilted her head and grinned his way. "For not making me clean the dust bunnies from your closet or polish your—as you put it—shit kickers."

He laughed and looked up at the falls. "The day isn't over yet."

"Still have plans for me, cowboy?"

Mesmerizing blues slowly took in her smile. His own slowly faded to a wistful line. "I do, but I'm not sure you're ready to hear them."

Her heart beat heavy with the rhythm of hope, but her mind snuck back in with an arsenal of memories, reminding her it wasn't wise to see too much into things. His thoughtful expression was probably no more than a trick of coincidence. Today was magical, and she'd treasure it forever, but she'd mark it for what it was—a beautiful day never meant to last forever.

Chapter Eleven

The metallic drone of a plane buzzed loudly from outside.

"Must be Garrett." Grace placed her dust rag down on the end table before following her grandmother out of the living room and then out the front door.

Garrett's blue and red bush plane was already fast on its way toward the hills, swaying its wings in the form of a wave.

"We must have missed the flyby." Her grandmother waved her arms high in the air as though there was some hope she'd be spotted. Out in the yard, Jenny and Doc did the same, and farther out near the pens, no less than a half-dozen cowboy hats waved above the hoots and hollers of a rowdy crew.

Something in the moment sent a mad rush of warmth surging through Grace's soul. She'd missed the caring and camaraderie of the ranch. She'd missed home.

When not even a speck remained to be seen of the plane, the hats lowered, Jenny wrapped her arms around her husband and cuddled into his side. Grace and her grandmother shared a smile then headed back inside.

"It was nice to see you and Garrett doing so well." Grams picked up the dust rag she'd left lying on the mantel and turned back to her. "Are you doing as well as you seem?"

"I am," she answered instinctually and then gave it more thought. Facing her demons hadn't been easy, but facing the facts had actually proven a relief. "Garrett and I were friends first. Once we talked things through, it was surprisingly easy to fall back into the role. I imagine the four years that have passed can be thanked for a lot of it."

"Time is a powerful healer, but forgiveness is about the heart. I'm proud of you, Grace."

"Thanks, Grandma." Her grandparents' approval meant a lot to her. She smiled, picked up her own dust rag, and happily got back to work.

They'd started their day early, wanting to get a number of chores done so they'd have plenty of time to prepare for the Baxter's social and dance taking place that evening. After they finished the living room, they'd be officially done.

Picking up a silver-framed photo of herself and her husband, Grams gently wiped clean its glass and border, studying the picture with somber eyes.

Grace paused in her polishing. "Are you okay?"

"He did all right without me." Her grandmother placed the photo back on the mantel then turned and smiled. "I always pictured him in chaos, moping around in a den of despair, missing me horribly." She laughed and looked away. "But that simply wasn't the case."

Grace followed her grandmother's gaze to the next frame on the mantel, inside lay a picture of her grandfather, Phil, and Mac. They were standing on some unfamiliar shore, holding up an impressive line of fish. The photo was new to her, taken some time during her and her grandmother's absence.

Gram's smile faltered as she studied the three

215

smiling faces. "He did just fine all on his own."

"Even the capable get lonely, Grandma. He missed you. That's all that matters."

"Yes, I see that now, and I should have seen it much sooner—the fact that he called all the time—the fact he purposefully baited me to keep me on the line."

"He's much better with ornery than open," Grace acknowledged.

Grams looked back her way and grinned. "He is, isn't he?"

Shrugging her shoulders, she smiled. "I think it's a man thing."

Still holding the polish firmly in her hand, her grandmother moved across the room to look out the window toward the yard where most of the men were working. "I've missed this."

"Me, too."

It wasn't the first time Grace had acknowledged the same. She now realized she'd missed Buster's Prairie a great deal. Looking back, she was surprised she'd been able to stay gone so long. The hurt she'd carried around as a shield all those years had done more than its job, shielding her not only from the pain, but also blinding her to the truth. Everything that she'd loved about the ranch was still here. It was still home and always had been.

Continuing on with their work, Grace and her grandmother moved silently through the rest of the room. When they were done, they took a seat beside each other on the couch, sighed, and plopped up their feet on the recently polished coffee table.

"Looks good." Grace studied the new shine of the room. "Well, Cinderella, now that we've finished our chores, we can prepare for the ball."

Resting her head back against the sofa, her grandmother laughed. "Sure wish I had a fairy godmother who could wave a magic wand and deliver me polished and shined."

"If you find one, be sure to ask for a luxury carriage with cheerful coachmen."

Grams shot her an amused grin, and they both burst out laughing. There'd be no jubilant escorts for them. Instead, they'd be riding to the ball inside a truck full of roughnecks, all not entirely pleased to find themselves heading to a dance.

Still smiling, Grace rested her head on her grandmother's shoulder. "Has Grandpa been grumbling?"

Grams silently thought it over. "You know, surprisingly, he's actually seemed a bit excited."

She grinned. "He's probably glad to be taking his girl."

"Maybe he is." Her grandmother wrapped her arm around her. "What would you think about your grandfather and me getting back together? It would mean I'd be staying here at the ranch."

Lifting her head, she gave a wide smile. "I'd think it a very good idea. Though, of course, I'll miss you terribly when I get back to Vancouver."

"Vancouver? You wouldn't have to go back to Vancouver. You could stay right here."

"I'd have to leave eventually, Grandma. I have to work. And in truth, the ranch doesn't need me. Mac and Grandpa have been doing a wonderful job all on their own."

Her grandmother threw back her head and laughed.

"Oh, Grace, a very wise young woman once pointed out to me that even the capable get lonely."

"Grandpa will have you."

"I'm not talking about your grandfather, Grace Elizabeth. I'm talking about that handsome young man who'll eventually be taking his place."

"Mac? You think Mac's going to keep me around just for my company?"

A bright pink covered softly wrinkled cheeks. "Well, not only for your company."

"Grandma!"

"Oh, Grace, old eyes aren't good for much, but they're pretty handy for seeing the forest through the trees. That young man has plans for you that have nothing to do with office work. Certainly you've seen it?"

She had seen it. Felt it. He was attracted to her, desired her, but that didn't mean he planned to keep her. "I can't start thinking that way, Grandma, especially not with him."

"What do you mean *especially* not with him? Why not him?"

"I'm not going to plan my life around a man who's already found plenty of reasons for another to walk away from me. Think about it, Grandma. If he was able to talk Garrett into leaving me, how hard do you think it would be for him to convince himself to do the same?"

"Very hard, if he's already in love with you."

She patted her grandmother's knee then rose. "Mac Palmer is not in love with me."

"I wouldn't be so sure."

"That's because you're my grandmother, and you do love me." Grace offered her hands to Grams to help her off the couch.

Taking them, she scooted herself to the edge and then stood. "Promise me one thing, will you, dear?"

"If I can."

"Give your heart the credit it's due. Heads can get muddled by all sorts of false perceptions, but hearts never do. They are nothing if not true."

"And fragile," Grace added. "There's a reason I try to rule my heart with my head these days, especially where Mac is concerned. I can hardly dismiss a past with so many warnings it practically cries *hazard*."

"Have you ever considered that maybe the reason Mac was so sure you were wrong for his brother was because he's so certain you're right for him?"

Grace stared back at her in surprise. "Grandma, have you been paying any kind of attention?"

She only grinned. "Better attention than you, I would say. And if I'm not mistaken, whether you want it or not, your heart's already invested." Patting Grace's hand, she nodded toward the stairs. "In case our fairy godmother gets lost, I think we'd better start getting ready."

Grace moved up the stairs beside her in a bit of a daze. Her grandmother was right—her heart was already invested. She'd let down her guard and let hope filter in, and hope was a tricky thing. No one knew that better than she. It built false bridges going nowhere and created promising mirages in relationships doomed for failure.

Stopping at the top of the stairs, she stared down toward Mac's room. She'd been a fool to believe she could control her feelings for him. She'd run from them, hid from them, denied them.

The only thing she'd never done was face them.

She was in love with Mac Palmer, and there was a good chance she always had been.

****

Mac parked the truck in a field full of others. From the looks of things, Claire and Tess had done a nice job of rounding up a good-sized Texas hoedown. It would most likely make for a long night after an already long day. "All right, folks," he said, "this taxi leaves at midnight. Anyone not out here finds another ride home."

"If there's a bus less crowded, I'm on it."

Looking up into the rearview mirror, he caught sight of Grace sitting on Phil's lap, looking anything but pleased.

It had been a matter of designated drivers. There had only been two, him and Jarrod, and the latter had left earlier with Tagger and Brody. They were making a wide swing around Amarillo to pick up their ladies. The only rig left had filled up fast. Lance, Mick, and Phil in the truck's back; him, Eldon, and Patsy sitting in front. There really hadn't been another seat. So, after much complaining and rearranging, Grace, the smallest and most nimble of their crew, had taken the first lap offered.

"Sorry to burst your bubble," he said, catching her attention, "but the only other bus isn't any less crowded and will be taking a detour."

"We need another rig," she complained, "one that actually runs. That old clunker in the barn isn't much use when it's always sitting up on bricks. Pretty soon, we're going to have to push it to get it anywhere."

"That old clunker's been with me since I came to

the ranch," Eldon said in the truck's defense.

"Not a selling point, Grandpa." She patted his shoulder then pushed open the back door.

Lance leaned forward as she moved to exit. "Don't forget you promised me a dance or two."

"Hey, I'll take one of those," Mick piped in.

"You've got it." Grace scooted off Phil's lap to jump down onto the gravel.

Leaving the keys dangling from the transmission, Mac hurried from the cab to join her on the ground. At the rate things were going, if he didn't get his bid in now, he might just lose out.

She watched him step down before walking straight past him. "I noticed you didn't request a dance. Card already full, Palmer?"

Following her around the truck's hood, he stopped right behind her as she waited for the others still making their way out of the truck. "Jealous?"

She tossed him a smirk over her shoulder. "I've seen you dance, remember? I'm really more relieved."

"Is that so?" He smiled, knowing her well enough to know it was her pride talking. "Give me another chance, sweetheart. I've come up with a few new moves. I think you'll be impressed."

A smile flickered across her lips. "I wouldn't be so confident. You had a long ways to go, and you've had very little time to get there."

Staring into her breathtaking blue eyes, enjoying the tilt of her lips, lips he knew to be sweeter than the first burst of a freshly ripened berry, he wanted desperately to kiss her. "Save a dance for me, and I'll prove it to you."

"I'll have to check out those new moves of yours

first."

"By that time, it might be too late. I may have been discovered and my dance card truly filled. Better stake your claim now, twinkle toes."

"All right, one dance."

"One! I'm worth more than one."

She bit into her lip, fighting a more boisterous smile that eventually broke free. "You think you're special, don't you?"

Feeling a bit uncertain, he pushed back his hat. "I hope so."

Gravel snapped and crunched behind them. "I don't know about anyone else," Phil said, slapping his hand down on Mac's shoulder, "but I'm heading for the chow line. I can smell the drippings of ribs on a barbie, and I have no intention of waiting around to find those babies gone."

Mick sniffed the air. "You don't get a better *come hither* than that, folks." Smacking the back of his hand against Lance's chest, he pulled the cowboy's attention away from the homestead's back door where Tess had disappeared with an empty platter. "You comin'?"

"Huh? Oh, yeah, yeah I'm coming." Lance placed the hat in his hands back on his head then stepped forward to lead the group around the other trucks and toward the back gate.

Mac glanced back to the Baxter's door and smiled. It looked like Tess had managed to turn the cowboy's head after all. There was another ranch hand he'd likely be losing. Once a cowboy's head got turned, there wasn't much hope. And didn't he know it.

He turned and focused back in on Grace.

Currently jousting and speed-walking with Mick

and Lance in some kind of comical race toward the chow line, she still managed to take his breath away. When exactly was it that he'd fallen so madly in love with her? It was starting to feel as though he always had been. Every memory he held of her seemed so clear, so alive, so much more than any other.

What would he do without her?

His heart squeezed. It suddenly became very difficult to breathe.

No!

He forced the thought away. Life without Grace was something he never again wanted to imagine.

****

The barn doors stood wide open. The light from inside was bursting out like a beacon along ocean shores. Inside the barn, white strings of light hung in a huge circle above haystacks covered with burlap and being used as seating. Standing mid-circle, a makeshift band boomed out a nice mix of old and new country songs. Impressive for what it was—a group of musician friends who simply enjoyed getting together on such occasions and entertaining a crowd.

Tables for dining were lined up one after another right outside the barn doors. Most now stood empty, left with only scattered and forgotten plates nearly wiped clean. That's where Grace chose to make herself useful, helping Tess and Savannah clear away the remains.

"I hear there was a high-stakes bull ride at Buster's Prairie yesterday," Savannah said as she worked to clear the next table over.

"It's true." Grace leaned across hers to collect a couple plates on its opposite side. "I should have known dangling a challenge in front of a cowboy would prove a bad idea."

"Story has it the cowboy let you off easy." Tess smiled her way before tossing an armful of used paper plates and plastic utensils into the trash.

"He did, and believe me, I feel quite fortunate. The last I'd heard his list of *to-dos* had hit a second page."

Her two new friends exchanged knowing looks.

"Care to share your thoughts?" She moved with her load of used goods to the trash.

Savannah followed behind. "There are rumors circulating of a romance blossoming between the two of you."

Dropping her load into the black bin, Grace eyed her warily. "And by 'circulating' I assume you mean from Jarrod to you?"

"Well, yes, but Tess has also heard the rumors."

Grace turned to the redhead who was now glaring at Savannah. "I told Lance I wouldn't say anything," she reprimanded.

She merely shook her head and walked back toward the table. "And men say it's women who like to spread gossip."

Savannah gave a funny snort. "Right. We all know the…" She paused, looking over Grace's shoulder. "There's Mac now."

And just like that, the two other women disappeared.

Talk about clearing a room. She turned to find the cowboy heading her way.

"Ready for that dance, Grace?"

Ready and willing.

The man couldn't be more handsome. His long,

muscle-clad torso sported denim better than any ad she'd ever seen, and his rugged good looks and killer smile could knock the good angel right off any woman's shoulder. She didn't even care if the man couldn't dance.

"Eager to prove your moves?" She played it cool as she walked his way, not an easy task when her blood was pumping to the tune of *Zip-a-Dee-Doo-Dah*.

"I have every intention of sweeping you off your feet." His smile grew wider as he watched her approach.

She stopped right in front of him. "Well then, I better take a moment to call my insurance agent and make sure I'm covered here in the States."

Wrapping his arms around her, he pulled her close. "Oh, don't you worry, sweetheart, I've got you covered." As though it were the most natural thing in the world, he led her toward the dance floor.

Inside the barn and near the refreshments table, Tess and Savannah stood huddled in a little circle with Jarrod and Lance. Yep, the rumor mill would have her and Mac bound and headed for the chapel before they even made it to the dance floor. That's how things worked in this isolated part of the country. It didn't take much to become the main event, and romance was a topic that basically flew without wings.

The quick-tempo of a popular favorite started to play as they made it to the floor's center. Much to her surprise and delight, Mac did indeed know a thing or two about swing dancing. Soon, they were heel-toeing, scooting, swaying, and swinging to the beat. Over all, they moved well together—gliding easily around the other couples while laughing, playing, and maybe once or twice making fools of themselves.

The song faded to gone, and the band announced they were taking a break. *Play* was hit on the boombox behind them and soon a much quieter song filled the gap left behind.

Grace smiled up to Mac. "I'll give it to you, Palmer. You definitely can dance. What happened at the falls? I think you held out."

"It was the pressure. I panicked." He shot her a mischievous grin. Taking her hand in his, he wrapped his free arm around her waist and pulled her against him. "One more?"

"Sure." She eyed the other couples around them. The ladies, all wrapped in their men's arms, rested their heads against their partners' comfortable chests. She would have liked to have done the same, but she was still uncertain enough of where they stood that she hesitated.

With his touch heating her flesh and sparking her imagination in dangerous ways, she felt the need to fill the silence. "Savannah seems nice." It was the best she could come up with.

"Yes, she is. A really nice lady. I'm guessing it won't be long before I lose myself that ranch hand." He looked across the room to where Lance and Tess were huddled together in a corner. He sighed. "Probably two."

Grace laughed, leaning back to look into his eyes. "Poor, Mac. Cupid is really playing havoc with your ranch."

He shot her a weary glance. "You can say that again. Do you know what your grandfather suggested earlier?"

"Grandfather? No, what?"

"He suggested we host our own annual shindig. Can you imagine?" His look of incredulity was nothing short of adorable.

"Oh, the horror!" She gasped, playing along with his outrage.

He grinned. "You mock me now, but wait until the planning actually begins, you'll see all the hard work such a festivity brings. It's brutal—all the planning, preparing, clean up." Shaking his head, he pulled her back against him. "And tell me it doesn't have your grandmother written all over it."

"Every square inch." Looking away to all the familiar faces, she took a deep breath and sighed. "It's not a bad idea, reciprocating with our own entertainment now and again. Good relations are a strong plus for any business, and out here, good friends are more valuable than gold."

She turned back to find him staring thoughtfully her way.

"What?"

"Sometimes you amaze me. That's all." He pulled her close and kissed her forehead.

Sometimes he amazed her, too.

****

The evening turned to midnight way too fast. Between promised dances, old friends and new, Grace never again found herself back in Mac's arms. The disappointment was huge.

She had hoped perhaps they'd share a private moment back at the ranch, but her grandparents, far giddier than she'd ever seen them, had confiscated the evening right out from under them with excited recapitulations of the night's events. They had, for whatever the reason, been terribly reluctant to let the night end.

After nearly thirty minutes, well into the early hours of the morning, Grace made her excuses and headed to bed. As much as she wanted that moment alone with Mac, she simply couldn't keep going any longer.

Closing her bedroom door behind her, she stopped and leaned back against it.

What a night. Though well beyond tired, she doubted sleep would be peaceful. There were simply too many thoughts bouncing around in her head. The dance with Mac had been wonderful. Being held in his arms, as though she were right where she was supposed to be, had felt better than anything she could ever remember.

He'd held her as though he treasured her, adored her…loved her.

Loved her.

Closing her eyes, Grace moaned and let her head fall forward into her hands. "You're a fool, Grace Wade." After four long years of heartbreak rehabilitation, she'd returned to the ranch and immediately set herself up for another fall. Mac Palmer did not love her. How could he? He knew all her truths, all her faults.

Her chest tightened, giving her heart a painful squeeze.

Kisses, dances, cuddles, dreams of forever—she couldn't do it. She simply couldn't go through the pain of loving, hoping, dreaming, and ultimately losing it all again. And she would…eventually. He'd pushed her away before and more than once. Certainly, this time would prove no different.

If she didn't put the brakes on things now, she was going to end up right where she'd started—back in Canada. This time alone, and with a hole in her heart even bigger than before.

She sighed, knowing it wouldn't be easy to walk away. She was simply too attracted to the man—tall, cowboy sexy, ridiculously handsome—who wouldn't be? And when he was being agreeable, he could tip the scales of charming. Not just hard to resist, the man was impossible to resist. To her, he simply felt too right.

"Wrong." She pushed away from the door. She wasn't going to go there. No longer a naïve little girl counting on some fairytale, she was a grown, independent, capable woman, smart enough to do what was best for her and determined—so very determined—to never again be another's "mistake."

New resolve in place, Grace moved to her dresser, grabbed her hairbrush and pajamas, and then headed across the hall to the bathroom. By the time she'd changed, brushed her teeth, and cleaned her face, the halls and downstairs had all fallen silent.

Peeking out the bathroom door, she thought seriously about making her way down to the opposite end of the hall and knocking on the door to the right. She'd march her determined self inside Mac's room and give it to him straight—a nice, clean, we-can-still-be-friends kind of break.

Would he allow it?

She knew only too well, Mac had a knack for persuasion. He was good at getting what he wanted, and at the moment, it appeared he wanted her. He might try and change her mind.

A part of her maybe even hoped he would.

Stop it, Grace!

Her resolve was apparently a bit weak at the moment, probably because she was so tired. Yeah, that's what it was, she was just too tired. She'd get a good night's sleep then face him in the light of day when her senses were less likely to be swayed.

If only my heart didn't pitter-patter so excitedly at the very thought of being near him.

Disgusted with herself, she flicked off the bathroom light and went to step out into the hall. It was then the door opposite Mac's opened. Grace paused, hesitant to get caught in another round of *what-a-wonderful-night-it-was*.

She watched as her grandmother stepped out of the room and then instantly turned back and grabbed hold of the knob. Just when Grace thought she'd disappear back inside, she, instead, slowly and silently pulled shut the door.

Interesting.

Grace stepped farther back into the darkened bathroom, pulling the door as close to closed as she could while still peeking out.

Her grandmother looked down the hall to Grace's room then across the hall to Mac's. Apparently satisfied with the silence, she started down the corridor, taking small, measured steps. With her shoulders rounded and bunched up near her ears, she reminded Grace of a child sneaking down the stairs to catch Santa.

The floorboards released only a few hushed squeaks as she made her way forward, but with each low moan, the older woman paused, took a breath, and rebuilt her nerve.

She smiled, wondering what it was dear Grandma was up to.

Wait a minute.

Her grandmother's eyes told the tale—gazing directly down the hall to her husband's door. She intended to brave what Grace had not dared. She was going for her man.

Wanting to laugh, cry, and rejoice all at the same time, she managed to hold herself together as her grandmother tiptoed directly past the bathroom's door.

Way to go, Grams. Grandpa was in for one heck of a surprise.

From the stairs sitting midway down the landing, came the pounding of boots taking the steps two at a time. Grace could no longer see, but she knew those steps well.

Her grandmother gasped.

"Sorry, Patsy," Mac said, "I didn't mean to startle you."

Grams laughed nervously. "That's all right, dear. I was merely surprised. I thought everyone had gone to bed."

"I'd headed that way earlier," he explained, "but I heard Jarrod pull up right as I hit the stairs and decided I better go out and make sure everyone made it home all right."

"Good idea." Her grandmother's voice was definitely a tad shaky. "I take it everyone is back and well?"

"And completely worn out. It's been quite an evening for all of us."

There was a long pause.

"Were you headed downstairs?" Mac asked, obviously a bit concerned. "Is everything all right? Can I get something for you?"

"No. No." The older voice rang a bit higher than normal. "I'd just been in the restroom getting ready for the evening. I was heading back to my room when I heard footsteps on the stairs. You know me." She laughed nervously. "I like to know what's going on."

Grace almost gasped. It was the first outright lie she'd ever heard her grandmother tell. It made her want to…to…well, giggle. She covered her mouth and stepped farther back into the room.

Outside the door "good nights" were exchanged. A couple seconds later, the bathroom door pushed open, and the light flicked on.

Mac spotted Grace and took a step back, his blue eyes opening wide. "What?"

Lifting her finger to her lips, she shushed him. He stared at her a moment longer before looking out the door to where her grandmother had stood.

He shut the door tight and turned the lock before taking the two steps that brought him beside her so he could whisper, "I thought Patsy said—"

"She lied." Grace grinned as she threw her grandmother under the proverbial bus.

A heavy crease formed between his brows. Reaching behind his head, Mac massaged his neck. "Why would she do that?"

"I'm not a hundred percent positive, but I think she was headed for my grandfather's room."

He blinked. Smiled. "I see. And you're hiding in here in the dark because…?"

"I didn't want to interfere with the magic."

"The magic," he repeated, staring back to the door. "I think maybe I screwed things up."

"Not for long." She moved past him to the tub. Reaching inside, she turned on the shower then tiptoed to the door and pressed her ear against it.

Mac grinned and followed suit. Sure enough, the squeaking of boards, this time a bit louder and ringing of determination, sounded outside the door. Another couple seconds and a knock came from farther down the passage. Muffled voices sounded. Laughter, then the door shut.

"Way to go, Patsy." Mac echoed her thoughts.

She looked up and smiled. "They're going to be okay this time. I just know it."

His piercing blue eyes, bright and soulful, gazed at her as though she were his everything. "They will be." Lifting a hand, he brushed a couple stray hairs back away from her eyes. "Eldon's smartened up this round. He knows what it is he has and how much he has to lose." Mac swallowed as he gently caressed her cheek. "Believe me, this time, he's never letting her go."

Those eyes were going to be the end of her—so deep, so passionate, so full of promise. She could almost believe he was talking about the two of them.

"Mac, I—"

His hands cupped her face as his gaze shifted to her lips.

A pulse beat rapidly just below her lobe. It was her turn to swallow. "I…I think we should—"

"Yes?" His lips were now moving toward hers.

"I think we should—"

Time moved slow when viewed through her excitement, but so did the kiss which finally silenced her thoughts as well as her words. She never wanted the stolen kiss to end. His lips felt too good against hers, his touch too exhilarating. There was nothing in the world that could feel any better.

For the first time since their trip to the falls, she relaxed and let pleasure serenade her into a beautiful, anxiety-numbing state of acceptance. For now or for forever, at the moment, she didn't care. It simply felt amazing. She would take what she could get and live the dream for just this one night. But tomorrow…

He pulled away. "Any chance you'd care to go for a walk?"

She blinked. "A…walk?"

"Yeah." He took a deep breath then nodded. "It's a great night—the stars are out, everything's peaceful."

Grace smiled. "That's because everyone's sleeping."

His lips twitched with amusement. "Scared of the dark, Wade?"

He was hard to resist in this mood. He was hard to resist period.

"Not scared of nothing, Palmer."

But her smile faltered. It was a lie. The idea of once again leaving the ranch broken, scared her to death.

****

Their steps fell near silent against the dirt paths that lined the ranch. Yet the only sounds louder were the moos from cattle grazing on distant hills and the songlike chirps of crickets calling for their mates. It was the perfect opportunity to tell Grace what was on his mind, but Mac wasn't finding it easy. Something was off. He wasn't sure what it was, but he had a good-sized feeling she was getting ready to fly. Something had spooked her. He only wished he knew what.

She looked up to the sky. "It's beautiful out tonight."

Thin, white clouds dangled in scarce patches across a dark-blue canvas speckled with stars. "It doesn't get any better." He stopped and turned to face her. As beautiful as the night might be, it held no comparison to Grace. Even in the baggy old sweats she'd tossed on over her pajamas, she was still a sight to behold.

He moved to wrap his arms around her, but she instantly dropped her gaze and took a step back.

"Look, Mac," she said, never quite meeting his eyes. "I think maybe we should slow things down a bit, take some time to think things through."

He knew she didn't mean it. It was just her running scared. But the words still reached straight into his chest and squeezed around his heart.

Distance—she's already making room for takeoff.

"What's changed, Grace?"

"What do you mean?"

Letting out a weary breath, he shook his head. Of course she wouldn't make it easy. "Come on. Don't pretend like you don't know. There's something between us, something pretty damn terrific, if you ask me. Why are you suddenly backing away? What's changed?"

"Nothing." A crease formed between her brows as sadness filled her eyes. "Nothing has changed. That's just it." She moistened her lips and looked down to the ground. "I'm still the same *me* I've always been, maybe a bit stronger, maybe a bit wiser, but under it all, still the same old Grace."

He shrugged. "What's wrong with that?"

She looked up, her deep blue eyes now shining with unshed tears. "I'm still the same Grace who drove you crazy, still the same Grace with dreams of marriage and family and happily-ever-after, still the same Grace who…" She swallowed hard and went on, "who never quite measured up."

It took him aback.

Things had been going so well as of late, he'd figured they'd finally jumped that particular hurdle—the one that always sat dead center any distance between them—their past. But like a stubborn weed, it just kept rearing its ugly head.

They'd never be able to yank its roots, but they could dang sure see it grew in a better direction.

Stepping forward, he reached for her hands, but she pulled them behind her.

"The same old Grace, huh?" He folded his arms across his chest and leaned back on his heels.

A tear fell, but still she lifted an obstinate chin and nodded.

"I see." He studied her closely. "The same old Grace who loved to run around the yard chasing dandelion seeds?"

"Same girl."

"The same old Grace who's too damn stubborn to back down from anything, and I do mean *anything*?"

She pursed her lips for several long seconds, but eventually replied, "Yep, that's me."

"The same Grace who used to leave chocolate kisses beside my horse gear then hide inside the barn and wait for me to find them?"

Her mouth dropped with surprise. "You knew?"

"Of course I knew. Just like I knew years later it was you who threw the red dish cloth in with my briefs."

She had the decency to blush. "Oh."

"Yeah. I had to wear those pink briefs for nearly two weeks before the new ones arrived."

"You'd called me a girl," she said in her own defense.

"You were and are a girl."

"It was the tone."

"I see. That Grace?"

She took a deep breath and let it out slowly. "'Fraid so."

He took a step closer, causing her to startle. "Are you still the same Grace who used to run around the yard, spreading her arms, declaring her love for the ranch and all the souls who lived here?"

She cringed and closed her eyes. "Stupid."

Mac wrapped his arms around her. "Adorable."

Her lips trembled as he leaned down to hover right above them.

"It's still you?"

"Still me."

"Good, because that Grace..." He paused to softly kiss her. "That Grace I love."

Deep blue eyes opened wide. She blinked. "You...you love?"

"Every inch of her stubborn, occasionally ill-behaved, beautiful, lovable hide." He kissed her again. "I love you, Grace. I love everything about you—from your soft heart to your incredibly sharp wit. I love the way you tempt me, try me, test me to my limits. I love your laugh, your smile, and even that sassy little snarl where your lip curls and your eyes throw fire. I love *you*, and everything that makes up who you are." He could see in her eyes she wanted to believe him, but she was struggling all the same.

Finally, she took a deep breath and asked, "You...you don't think you'll change your mind?"

"Change my mind? About loving you?"

"You wouldn't be the first."

He held on tight when she would have moved away. "Never. I'll never change my mind. I will love you, Grace Wade, until the day I die. I'm never letting you go. And I mean that literally." He smiled. "I still have your passport."

Happiness and disbelief fought a duel inside Grace's head, but it was delight that pushed them both into the background. Mac was kissing her again and kissing her with a passion that shined light on the truth.

He loved her; truly *loved* her.

And heaven knew how much she loved him.

Wrapping her arms around him, she finally let go—let go of the hurt, of the sorrow, of the doubt. She had never been destined for Garrett Palmer. Her heart and her destiny had always belonged to his brother.

When they finally parted, he cupped her face in his hands. "This might sound a bit rushed, but it's only because I can't wait to make you mine. I want you bound and obligated before you ever have a chance to run away again. I want to know you're here and here forever."

She felt her knees weaken, her heart flutter. "O...kay."

"Okay, you'll marry me?"

Her breath caught as her heart attempted to leap

right out of its holder. She held tighter to his arms and stammered, "D-did you ask?"

A bright smile spread across his face. "Come with me."

The next thing she knew, they were back at the house.

He stopped in the middle of the yard and pointed down. "Wait right here." Then he took off across the yard.

"Where are you going?"

"To my mom's. I'll be right back."

"To your—"

He was already gone.

A couple minutes later, the veranda light turned on. The front door opened. The screen door creaked. Her grandfather stepped out. Shading his eyes against the glare of the light, he looked out into the yard. "Grace?" He scowled. "What in tarnation are you doing outside?"

The door opened wider behind him. Her grandmother stepped out and around him. "Grace, dear, is something wrong?"

The lights from the yard behind theirs flipped on.

"I'm fine, really." She wasn't cold, but she started to shiver. "I was just out for a walk."

"At this time of night?" Her grandfather stepped up to stand beside his wife. "By yourself? Are you crazy?"

"She's with me." Mac rounded the corner with his mother and Doc following close behind him.

Grace's shivering form started to sway. It was all starting to feel a bit surreal.

Holding a small box in his hand, he headed her way.

Behind him, Jenny stopped and covered her

smiling lips with her hands. Doc stepped up beside her and wrapped his arm around her shoulders.

"Well, I'll be," Gramps declared from the top of the veranda.

Mac stopped right in front of Grace and dropped to one knee. Her heart took a leap, sending her pulse racing and thoughts into an entirely different orbit.

Can this really be happening?

"Grace Elizabeth Wade." He took her hand in his. "You are the best thing…the *very best thing* that has ever happened to me."

She caught her breath and held it in disbelief. He'd said the words. Mac Palmer had actually said the magic words.

"I love you," he added, squeezing her hand. "Please, say you'll marry me."

The dinner bell on the veranda rang fiercely into the night. Grace and Mac looked back to find her grandparents with an arm wrapped around each other, wide smiles on their faces, and ringing the bell as though their house was on fire.

The lights from the bunkhouse and Phil's house flicked on. Soon, the grounds were flooded with worried faces and bare feet.

Grace officially felt ridiculous.

"What is it?" Mick asked, being last to arrive.

Phil nudged his shoulder then pointed to the lawn's center.

"Well, go ahead," her grandfather hollered. "Give the man an answer."

"I…" She hesitated, still not believing it real.

"This isn't another trick, is it?" Brody asked.

Tagger smacked his arm. "Pay attention."

"Grace?" Mac vied for *her* attention.

She looked down into his hopeful face and nearly cried with happiness. "Is this real?"

He smiled and opened the box. A single solitaire sat in the center of a beautifully etched silver band. "It was my mother's from my father. She gave it to me and asked only one thing—that I give it to a woman worthy of all my heart. That's you, Grace. You have it all. If you say yes, you'll make me the happiest man alive."

Grace fell to her knees. Taking his handsome face in her hands, she nodded. "Yes, I'll marry you. I love you, too. Every square, stubborn inch of—"

Pulling her tightly into his arms, he kissed the words right off her lips as hoots and hollers erupted around them.

Chapter Twelve

"Oh, honey, you look beautiful." Grace's mother stepped back to take in the full effect—the vintage allure of a classical silk and lace gown, the long flowing veil, the elegantly lifted hair. Her eyes began to water. "Absolutely stunning."

"She's right, Grace." Jenny searched her purse for a new hanky. "You're going to take my son's breath straight away." Her lips quivered as she looked up. "I'm so happy."

Pulling tissues from a nearby box, Grams held them out to the two anxious mothers. They both sniffed, took the tissues, and dabbed at their eyes as they pulled themselves together.

Grace smiled at her grandmother. "No tears, Grandma?"

"There's too much happiness in my heart for tears." She took a few more tissues and held them clutched at her side all the same.

Waving her hands in front of her eyes, Grace looked up, trying desperately not to cry. It was the first time she'd worn mascara in years, and she was already starting to question her judgment. "Has anyone checked? Are you certain he's there?"

She couldn't help but be leery. The last wedding she'd shown for, the groom had gone missing. And though she knew Mac deeply loved her, the memory of that moment proved a strong one to shake.

"He's here, Grace." Her grandmother took her hand. "He always has been—standing right beside you, making sure you get it right."

"He has, hasn't he?" She squeezed the aged hand then glanced nervously toward the door. "Are they ready for me yet?"

Her mother walked across the room to peek out the front door and exchange words with the two men waiting outside. "They're ready," she said after stepping back inside, "and there's a very handsome groom looking eager to get it started."

"Then I better hurry up." Grace couldn't wait herself. She was more than ready to start her new life with Mac at her side.

The three older women left her with kisses and hugs. As they walked out, her grandfather and father stepped in.

Her father's face lit with pride. "Look at our girl, Dad. Isn't she beautiful?"

"Mac Palmer is a lucky man." Gramps tugged at his tie. "Let's get this wedding moving. This dang blasted thing is about ready to choke me."

Grace grinned. He'd done a lot of growing, but there was only so much you could ask of one ornery old man. "Come on, Gramps," she said, linking her right arm through his, "I need you alive when you give me away."

Her father chuckled and held the door open, then wrapped his arm through her left as they passed. "Happy, baby girl?"

"Happier than I ever imagined."

And she was. She had it all—a family that loved

her, a beautiful home, and the heart of a man she loved with every bit of her own.

Seconds later, escorted by the two men who had for so many years been her anchor, she headed toward the aisle and the man who, from there on after, would be her world.

It was a lovely day, the sky as blue and the hills as magnificent as she could ever remember. She and Mac had decided there was no place they'd rather be married than there at the ranch. Their aisle would be the carpet of grass that had cushioned their steps for so many years. The altar would be the old eucalyptus that held the swing where they'd someday watch their children play. The distant hills and miles of open range would be their background, and those who had shared their journey, who had stood by them as friends and loved them as family, would be the only other decoration the day would need.

Everyone stood as she approached. Grace could feel their eyes upon her, but the only eyes she looked for were waiting at the end of the aisle, staring right at her, watching her as though she were already his. And she was. God knew it as did everyone there. For years and for forever it simply was and would be, the incredible man at the end of the aisle.

I love you—his lips formed the words that reached across the short distance to warm her heart and hurry her steps.

Her father held her back. "You're still mine for the moment," he said, but seeing her face, he merely kissed her forehead and let go of her arm. "All right, little one."

Still holding her other, her grandfather chuckled

and let go. "I hate to say it, but you're just like me, kid." Leaning forward, he kissed her cheek. "Go get him, Gracie."

She kissed them both. "I love you so very much." Then, lifting the hem of her dress, she hurried the rest of the way down the aisle.

"I love you, too," she said, landing in Mac's arms.

Their kiss was long and full of promise.

The priest cleared his throat. "Hey, you two, not yet."

Mac pulled away. "Sorry."

But the smile on his face showed no remorse at all, and made her grin all the wider.

She was right where she was supposed to be, right where destiny had planned. Together with Mac, now and forever, without a single regret in her heart.

A word about the author...

Amity Grays is a romance writer by night, accountant by day, and chocolate enthusiast 24/7. She lives in Southern Idaho with her husband, two daughters, two sweet dogs, and one snobbish cat who is under the mistaken impression she's royalty.

True to the nature of an accountant, Amity is a list builder, budget monitor, and proud owner of a 2005 Camry, which she's holding onto for another 120K miles because the salesman assured her she'd get 300K, and she feels the need to test his accuracy. On the flip side of her obsessive nature is a desire to let go—to spin a globe, point a finger, and explore the world.

http://www.amitygrays.com

Thank you for purchasing
this publication of The Wild Rose Press, Inc.

If you enjoyed the story, we would appreciate your
letting others know by leaving a review.

For other wonderful stories,
please visit our on-line bookstore at
www.thewildrosepress.com.

For questions or more information
contact us at
info@thewildrosepress.com.

The Wild Rose Press, Inc.
www.thewildrosepress.com

Stay current with The Wild Rose Press, Inc.

Like us on Facebook

https://www.facebook.com/TheWildRosePress

And Follow us on Twitter
https://twitter.com/WildRosePress

www.ingramcontent.com/pod-product-compliance
Lightning Source LLC
Chambersburg PA
CBHW070050260626
47160CB00004B/1153